Walk-In

VAL TOBIN

DEDICATION

Dedicated to Bob, Jenn, Mark, Chanelle, Savannah, and Jack

ACKNOWLEDGMENTS

Editing by Kelly Hartigan (XterraWeb) editing.xterraweb.com. Thank you, Kelly.

Thanks to Patti Roberts of Paradox (paradoxbooktrailerproductions.blogspot.com.au/) for the amazing cover.

Thanks also to Andrea Holmes; Diane King and The Hedge Witch; Val Cseh; Wendy Quirion; Michelle Legere; John Erwin; Jeff McQueen; Alis Kennedy; Newmarket: What's Happening group members, particularly Elizabeth Devry RN Con(C);
Any errors or departures from reality are mine and not the fault of any of the experts I consulted..

CHAPTER 1

Viktoria Kovacs's stomach lurched when she flipped over the Death card.

Hunched over the Celtic cross configuration of Tarot cards spread on the coffee table before her, she mentally slapped herself. Served her right for reading herself after a long and tiring Saturday doing readings for others.

Her job at The Green Witch, the new age store where she worked from Tuesday to Saturday, entailed doing psychic readings and manning the cash register when need dictated. Despite fatigue after the busy day, a sense of impending doom had compelled her to do a reading for herself.

Viktoria had barely kicked off her shoes before she'd sat down to it and now regretted the decision. The Tarot, of all things. What had possessed her to use the Tarot when she had oracle cards available?

Too late now. All she could do was take the bad news. She examined the spread, hoping to coax something uplifting from it. Hadn't she suspected it would be bad news? All day dread had hovered over her.

It had taken all her self-restraint to wait until she'd arrived home to break out the cards. Sure, she could have asked one of the other readers to do it for her, but then they'd know how frightened she'd become. They'd either not believe her, which would frustrate her, or they'd take her seriously, which would kick her terror up another notch.

Certain something horrific was coming, Viktoria came home to figure it out on her own. Now she sat staring at the Death spread.

The Death card didn't signify death, regardless of the implication inherent in its name. It meant change or renewal. Based on its position in the cross, though, the change it heralded had negative connotations. In the near future, a man would enter her life, and he would cause her harm. Family would influence the situation.

Viktoria gazed down and to the right, the stance she assumed when she

1

received clairvoyant information. She preferred to call the images received "impressions." They never appeared crisp and clear in her mind. She could describe what she saw in detail—could even draw it—but the image always hovered just outside of distinction.

This time, her face floated before her, but instead of mahogany waves, her hair was blonde and cut to shoulder length. Blood-red lips formed an "O" of amazement, and the deep brown eyes went wide.

The image vanished, replaced by another: A pen and paper.

Then that, too, disappeared.

A teak coffin, new and shiny. Gone.

Flashes of images flickered by so quickly she couldn't identify them.

Viktoria leaned back, breathless. Too fast. She couldn't understand what she'd seen.

Walter, her orange and white tabby cat, thumped into her lap, and she jumped.

After her heart stopped hammering, she stroked him, letting him settle his warm body on her thighs.

Should have used the oracle cards.

Again, she pushed the thought away. Regrets were useless and, in this instance, unnecessary. The oracle cards would help her get clarity as well as provide positive guidance. She scooped up the Tarot cards without completing the reading and set them aside.

As she tipped the cat from her lap and rose to get the other deck from her home office, her apartment buzzer sounded. Not expecting company, she froze.

An image of a swarthy man, face hidden in shadow, flashed into her mind's eye.

She considered ignoring the intercom, but when the buzzer went off again, she walked over to the door and pressed the speaker button.

"Yes?"

"Viktoria Kovacs?" The voice was soft, feminine, and tremulous.

"Yes?" Viktoria sucked in a breath. Her hands shook, and a knot formed in her stomach. The uneasiness that had plagued her all afternoon returned full force.

"May I come up?"

"Who are you?"

Silence, except for the slight static of the intercom, stretched out.

"Hello? Are you still there?"

A loud exhalation of breath came through the speaker. "It'll be easier to explain who I am if you let me come up."

Viktoria imagined buzzing the woman up and then opening the door to a home invasion.

"I don't think so." Too bad she couldn't see into the lobby and at least get a glimpse of the stranger. What if others were with her?

"Please. It's just me."

"Tell me who you are and what you want. You might be a jewel thief." Viktoria recalled a sitcom where one of the characters had let a jewel thief into the apartment building. No way would she buzz in a stranger.

But the woman had used Viktoria's first name, and that wasn't listed on the directory.

A light chuckle floated up through the intercom. "I'm not a jewel thief."

After a pause, the woman continued. "I'm sorry to tell you like this, Viki. I wanted to avoid it."

The woman paused again, and, in that quiet moment, the voice echoed in Viktoria's mind. Her heart thudded with recognition.

No. Impossible.

Breath held, Viktoria waited.

"I'm Eszter." A choked sob carried up to Viktoria, and she staggered away from the intercom as if she'd been struck.

The buzzer zapped again and again like an angry swarm of bees.

Viktoria pressed the intercom. "Eszter's gone."

"Please. Let me up. I'll prove it to you. Viki, please."

Numbness spreading over her, Viktoria released the intercom and pressed the button to open the lobby doors. In the ensuing silence, she backed against the wall and slid down to the floor.

CHAPTER 2

Numb, Viktoria lifted herself from the floor and stood waiting at the peephole. If that was truly Eszter on her way up, Viktoria would be able to tell at a glance even though they hadn't seen one another in five years.

Eszter was Viktoria's twin sister.

The walls and door of the apartment were well insulated and the hall carpeted. All was silent until the woman appeared before the peephole.

Even though she recognized Eszter, Viktoria squinted into the peephole, trying to improve the view. The face was unmistakeably Viktoria's duplicate, but the straw-coloured, shoulder-length bob was that of the woman whose image had flashed into her mind before.

With trembling hands and icy fingers, Viktoria unlocked the deadbolt and threw open the door. She stepped back, ushering Eszter inside, unsure whether they should hug or stand and stare at each other. Viktoria chose the latter, but Eszter chose the former.

Her body shuddering with sobs, Eszter grabbed Viktoria in a squeeze.

"Oh, my God. I can't believe I'm here. Viki, I'm so sorry. Please, you have to tell me if Mamma and Daddy are okay." Eszter pressed her face onto Viktoria's shoulder.

"Yes. We never stopped searching for you, Ess, but they're okay." Unaware she was doing it, Viktoria wrapped her arms around Eszter and kissed the top of her head. Tears streamed down Viktoria's face, but she wept quietly, holding back while Eszter let loose.

After a moment, they released one another, and Viktoria stepped back to study Eszter.

She appeared uninjured and well fed, and her long nails were the same blood red as her lips. The dress she wore, light and gauzy for the steamy July evening, screamed designer.

Wherever she'd been, she'd taken care of herself.

4

Anger worked its way through Viktoria.

The family had endured Eszter's sudden disappearance, a fruitless search by police and the local community, and five years of agony. Viktoria and her parents had continued to hunt long after the police had made it a cold case.

Voice choked with emotion, Viktoria said, "What happened? Why haven't you contacted us?" She forced herself not to scream accusingly, not to spew out all the hurt and rage churning inside her. Her sister had run away after all, leaving the family twisting in the wind.

Our lives went on hold, damn it. You had no right.

Best to leave that unspoken. For now. Let Eszter explain, and then Viktoria could unleash the tirade.

Eszter kicked off the high heels she wore—real leather from the look of them—and strode into the living room. She glanced around as she moved to the couch and curled up on it, her long, shapely legs tucking under her.

"I didn't run away, Viki. At least, I don't think I did." She dug through her purse. "I need a tissue." Eszter sniffled.

"Yes, of course. I'm sorry. I'm in shock." Viktoria inhaled deeply, three times, hoping to stop the tears that wanted to keep flowing and ease the pain in her chest. She grabbed a box of tissues from an end table and passed it to Eszter.

Viktoria sank into the armchair across from Eszter. "Searching for you became ingrained, you understand? I never go anywhere without hoping I'll spot you. God, Eszter."

Eszter blew her nose and nodded at Viktoria. "I don't remember leaving. I can't remember that day, or many days after. It's all a blank. My first recollection is of Niko." She paused and shook her head. "He's the man who found me. I was living in the streets. At least, he says I was."

Viktoria wanted to be patient, but Eszter's pauses and rambling narrative chafed her nerves. "Who's Niko? Why should you believe what he says?"

"He took me in." Eszter's gaze met Viktoria's. "He didn't kidnap me, Vik. He saved me. I was wandering around, nameless, homeless. I was on drugs. Two assholes attacked me. Niko caught them and intervened. He took me home and cleaned me up. I had no ID on me. He gave me a name, called me Talitha—someone he used to know. I remind him of her, he says. I think he loved her once. Still does, I guess."

"What happened to her?" The digression helped calm Viktoria's frazzled emotions. Nothing was more important right now than the answer to that question.

"I think she died. He doesn't talk to me much about his past."

"How did you remember?"

Fear, and then sorrow, flashed across Eszter's face. "It's bad, Vik. Bad for all of us."

The anxiety pouring from Eszter flowed into Viktoria.

Her voice a whisper, Viktoria said, "What is it? Just tell me."

Eszter hung her head. "I'm dying. Breast cancer. When I got the diagnosis, I remembered. The news hit me deep down, and I remembered Gramma had died at my age of breast cancer, and Auntie Joanna. It was like a dam burst then, and my name, you, where I came from—everything came back." She raised her head and met Viktoria's horrified gaze.

"Oh, God, Eszter." Viktoria rushed to Eszter, hugged her, and held her. Both were crying again, Viktoria silently, Eszter in heart-wrenching sobs.

"They could be wrong." Viktoria released her twin and, for a moment, let hope replace despair. "They get false positives all the time."

But Eszter shook her head, crushing the glimmer of light in Viktoria's heart. Eszter gripped Viktoria's hand, squeezing the fingers to the point of pain, but Viktoria ignored that.

"I've already gone for a second opinion. Besides, I discovered the lump myself. Even before I found it, I suspected something was wrong. I knew, Vik."

"There must be treatments. Breast cancer isn't a death sentence anymore. I know women who've survived it. You're not dying."

Again, Eszter shook her head, an almost imperceptible back and forth that had Viktoria's throat closing.

"It's metastasized. By the time they diagnosed me, it had already spread to the lymph nodes, and that's the kiss of death."

"So now what?" Viktoria steeled her heart for more horrible news.

"I've rejected treatment."

"What? Why?"

"What for? To destroy my body and endure pain and suffering just to prolong the inevitable? No, Vik." For the first time, anger replaced the grief in Eszter's voice.

This must have been an argument she'd had with others, probably that Niko person.

"Okay. What about alternative treatments? They're not as invasive, and if what you say is true, it can't hurt."

Eszter waved the suggestion away with a flick of a hand. "I've investigated. It's nonsense. I won't give myself false hope just to line some snake oil salesman's pockets."

"Don't think like that. It might work. People have cured themselves before." Perhaps one of the ladies at The Green Witch could help. They had a wealth of information on alternative therapies and numerous contacts with natural health practitioners.

Eszter's eyes narrowed and flashed with anger. "Name one person you know personally who cured their own cancer." She released Viktoria's hand.

Viktoria hung her head and flexed the numbness out of her fingers. "I can't, but that doesn't mean it's impossible."

"Forget it. Don't talk to me about voodoo crap. It's for gullible people who have more money than brains."

Viktoria's head snapped up, and she locked her gaze on Eszter's. "Stop it, Eszter. What a horrible thing to say."

How could Eszter believe that, when their family was the latest in a long line of witches and psychics? Herbal remedies had been the norm in their household when they were growing up, and most of them helped or even cured what ailed them.

An image of a grave popped into Viktoria's head, the headstone displaying Eszter's name. But the date on it was two weeks after Eszter had disappeared. Not wanting to deal with it right now, Viktoria pushed it aside. It didn't make sense, as was often the case with clairvoyant messages.

"Where's Niko now?" Viktoria lightened her tone, not wanting to argue. They'd been apart so long, fighting over anything, even something as important as Eszter's health, seemed self-indulgent.

"At our home. I wanted to meet with you alone before introducing him to the family. He offered to accompany me, for moral support, but I refused." She closed her eyes and gave a small sigh. "I wasn't sure how you'd take it, Vik. I was afraid you wouldn't recognize me."

"Wouldn't it have been easier on you if Niko were here?" A flutter of unease brushed Viktoria, and the headstone image flickered back into her head. Unable to push it aside this time, she struggled to sense the meaning. When she couldn't, she sent a request to her guides: *I don't understand. Please clarify.*

She opened herself up to receive another message, but Eszter leaped from the sofa. The image faded with the distraction, and Viktoria rose, panic striking her at the alarm on Eszter's face.

"What is it, Ess?"

"Nothing. It's okay. I'm sorry." Eszter sank back onto the edge of the sofa, back straight, feet planted on the floor, hands folded primly in her lap. She cleared her throat and raised her chin as though she'd made an important decision.

"I'd like you to meet me at Mom and Dad's tomorrow. You get there first and tell them I'm back. I'll bring Niko with me, but I don't want you all swooping down on him. He's done nothing wrong. He saved my life. I don't want anyone grilling him as though he's responsible for my disappearance."

"Do you expect us to jump to that conclusion even after explaining everything to me?" Viktoria sat again.

She shrugged. "I don't want anyone to make him think he's a suspect."

That would be up to the police. Viktoria kept the comment to herself.

She didn't want to upset Eszter, but Viktoria would make sure the investigating officers on the cold case would get updated. Let them figure out if Niko was responsible for what had happened to Eszter. If he'd had anything at all to do with the disappearance, they'd uncover it.

"Don't worry," Viktoria replied. "No one in the family will make him feel like a suspect." She averted her gaze as the image of Eszter's grave popped back into her head.

CHAPTER 3

Viktoria locked the door behind Eszter, who'd insisted she needed to get home to Niko. Eszter's contact information had been added to Viktoria's cell phone. If Eszter was a no-show tomorrow, Viktoria would know exactly where to send the cops this time.

The nagging feeling that Niko wasn't as Eszter portrayed him kept Viktoria tense and suspicious. How was it possible he'd never made the connection to the missing woman whose picture was all over the news and plastered on lampposts in their hometown of Newmarket, Ontario and the surrounding areas? Why hadn't he gone to the police to find out who she was?

Viktoria checked the time. Seven o'clock already, and she hadn't had any dinner yet. After the emotional upheaval of Eszter's return, Viktoria's stomach was in knots. Food would congeal in her gut, and she was afraid it would come right back up. She went into the kitchen, got some water, and then returned to the living room to retrieve her cell phone.

Her intuition was garbled. Try as she might, she couldn't get clarification on the headstone image, and nothing else about Eszter, her disappearance, or Niko came in. Perhaps a seasoned psychic and witch like Rowan would get better results. Viktoria called Rowan, The Green Witch's owner and Viktoria's best friend, and asked her to come over.

By eight o'clock, the two women were sitting in the living room. Viktoria had set a tray of tea and muffins on the coffee table, and while the cup of tea she sipped on soothed her, the muffin she chewed on sat in her stomach like a hairball.

"When Eszter first disappeared, what impressions did you get?" Rowan said.

"I didn't. Nothing came through no matter how hard I tried." Remembering that awful time brought back with it a sense of loss and bereavement. "We were terrified she was dead, but I couldn't verify it. At the time, I assumed grief and proximity to the situation blocked me ..."

"What are you thinking now?"

Viktoria shook her head. "Nothing concrete." She sighed. "Maybe we were right, and it was a matter of emotional involvement and trying too hard. But, even then, I couldn't shake the sense of being blocked."

Rowan frowned. "I read about it in the news." She picked up her cup of tea and sipped. When she set it down again, she said, "I've never told you this, because I thought it didn't matter, but I tried to connect to Eszter."

"You mean before I met you?"

Viktoria and Rowan had met two years before when Viktoria had applied to be a reader at The Green Witch. She'd impressed Rowan with her psychic abilities, and Rowan had hired her on the spot. They'd been not only coworkers but close friends ever since.

When Viktoria had told Rowan about her missing sister, Rowan had immediately tried to pull in information on the case but had received nothing substantial.

"Yes. I didn't tell you when we met, because nothing came of the information I got."

"But you got something? And didn't tell me?" Viktoria picked at the muffin on her plate, crumbling what was left between her fingers. "When I asked you to try, you said you couldn't get anything. Is that true?"

Rowan gently pried the muffin from Viktoria's fingers and set the plate and mess of crumbs on the table. She took Viktoria's hands in her own.

"I got something, yes, before I met you. I took the information to the police, but they never updated me after. When you and I met and you asked me to do the remote viewing for you, I did, and it went as I'd said. I received no useful information. I picked up less than I had when I first heard the news."

"What did you get the first time, Ro, and why didn't you tell me about it?"

Rowan sighed. "I'm sorry. Maybe I should have mentioned it, but three years had passed. The police hadn't found anything or contacted me for follow up, and I didn't want to upset you." She released Viktoria's hands. "I was obviously wrong, anyway. Eszter came back."

A lump formed in Viktoria's throat as the image of the headstone appeared in her mind's eye again. Breath held, she asked, "What did you see?"

"You have to understand, we hadn't met then. I only wanted to help."

"Rowan, I won't shoot the messenger. I understand how this stuff works. What did you get?"

"That someone had taken her, and she was in spirit." Rowan squeezed her eyes shut and shook her head, her long, red mane swishing behind her back.

"Okay." Viktoria exhaled. "She's back, so she's obviously not in spirit. You were right not to tell me. I was terrified of that and afraid we'd never find her body. If you'd told me that, it would have been a nightmare come true, and it would have been incorrect." Realizing there had to be something more, something Rowan still concealed, she added, "What was it you went to the police with, then?"

"Have you ever tried remote viewing?"

"Yes."

"Any luck?"

Restless, Viktoria rose and walked to the living room window. Daylight faded. The traffic on Davis Drive flowed steadily. A bus headed east disgorged two passengers at the bus stop and then continued along the bus lane.

Viktoria had tried remote viewing, which involved focusing on a target to receive psychic impressions, in her search for Eszter. "Some minor results. I'm only fair at it. I got nothing when Eszter disappeared. I couldn't feel her anywhere, even in spirit."

She turned back to face Rowan. "Tell me. What did you get?"

"I thought she was dead, remember, and that she'd been kidnapped. So I focused on who took her. I got that two people were involved—a man and a woman. But when I opened to receive more information, a location or a description, it shut down. All I got was a black wall. But there was power there, Vik, and I sensed strong interference." She rose, went to the window, and peered out. "Busy out there. That's why I prefer living in Sharon. Fewer people."

"You live on Leslie Street, Ro. It's just as busy."

"Not north of Green Lane."

"You're distracting me. Surely you didn't tell the police a powerful witch took her? Do you think a witch took her?"

Rowan paced between the window and the coffee table. "Not a witch, no. But someone with power. It felt more druidic than witchy—definitely not Wiccan. Wicca, as a religion, didn't appear until the 1950s. What I felt was much older." She stopped walking and put an arm around Viktoria. "I'm sorry, sweetie. Whoever took her did it with a purpose in mind." She hesitated.

"Sex? Did they take her for sex?" Panic edged Viktoria's voice, and she forced herself to take a deep breath. Eszter had returned, looking so good Viktoria had assumed Eszter had run away, causing the family needless worry and stress.

"Not sex, but I can't figure out what. It's not over, Vik. Don't trust Eszter or anyone she's associated with. I don't say these things lightly." Rowan turned to Viktoria, hugged her, and then stepped away. "When I walked in here tonight, I felt energy that wasn't you. Whatever or whoever it is, it feels sinister. Listen to me. Don't trust Eszter."

Anger percolated through Viktoria, and she stepped away from Rowan and frowned at her. "She's my twin. Missing for five years. I'm not turning my back on her."

"I'm not saying you should."

"She's dying." Viktoria's voice hitched as the tears flowed. "Eszter has breast cancer. I wasn't going to tell you. I don't know if she minds that I've said something, but I can't keep it inside. We lost her for five years, and now we'll lose her again."

"Oh, God, Viki. I'm so sorry." Rowan put an arm around Viktoria and guided her back to the couch.

"Sit."

When Viktoria sat, Rowan poured a fresh cup of tea. "Drink this," she said, holding out the cup and saucer.

Viktoria accepted the tea and sipped. It was still hot and soothed her insides. She stopped crying. "My parents will be devastated."

"Your parents are strong. They survived the last five years, and they'll cope with this. You all will. At least you have her back now. With Eszter here, you'll pull together as a family. And if conventional treatments aren't working, I'll refer her to some alternative practitioners."

Eyes tearing up again, Viktoria shook her head. "She won't do it. She's refusing all treatment."

When Rowan didn't reply, Viktoria glanced up.

Face white, Rowan's seafoam eyes met Viktoria's gaze.

Numb, Viktoria hugged herself. "What is it, Ro?"

Rowan opened her mouth to speak and closed it again. Finally, she said, "Oh, God, she's come for you." Rowan slid to the floor in a faint.

CHAPTER 4

Springing off the couch, Viktoria knelt beside Rowan who groaned and stirred the moment Viktoria touched her shoulder.

"Rowan, are you okay? What happened?"

"I don't—Viki." The words came out in bursts. "Sick."

Scrambling, Viktoria helped her friend to her feet and half-carried her into the bathroom. Rowan curled over the toilet, Viktoria holding Rowan's hair back while she retched.

"It's okay, Ro. I'm here."

"Oh, no—" Whatever Rowan wanted to say was cut off by another round of retching. When the worst of it subsided, she staggered to the sink. She splashed water on her face, rinsed her mouth, and accepted the towel Viktoria passed her.

Rowan breathed deeply and buried her face in the towel for a moment. When she looked up again, she said, "I'm so sorry. It hit me all at once."

Viktoria rubbed Rowan's back. "You'll be okay?"

"Yes. More embarrassed than anything else." Rowan blew out a long breath.

"I'll get you some water. Come on."

The women returned to the living room, and Rowan curled up on the couch while Viktoria grabbed her some water from the water purifier. When they were both settled, the heaviness and unease that had plagued Viktoria all day returned.

"What did you see?" Viktoria leaned back in her seat, fighting a trace of vertigo as she picked up on Rowan's energy.

"My third eye. I saw blood. There's danger around you, Vik, and it's coming from Eszter." Rowan rubbed between her brows at the point where her third eye, her psychic centre, was. "Damn. It's awful. It feels like something's crawling around in there." She set the glass of water on the

13

table and lay down on the couch.

Her breath came in short, shallow gasps. "I can't breathe. Please, help me clear my third eye."

Viktoria sat next to Rowan and covered her third eye with the palm of one hand. "Let me see. Relax."

"It's as if bugs are crawling in my third eye. Get them out, Vik."

"Okay. It'll be all right. Let me do this." Viktoria called on Archangel Michael and Archangel Raphael. "I'm working with the angels, okay?" Rowan didn't typically work with angelic energy, and Viktoria needed Rowan's permission to continue.

"Yes. Go ahead." Rowan closed her eyes and relaxed under Viktoria's hands.

In Viktoria's inner vision, an eye floated, open and bright, while tiny, black worm-like creatures spilled out of and away from it. She sent them into the earth to be transmuted into neutral energy. When the eye had cleared, Viktoria removed her hands.

"How does that feel?"

"Better. Oh, my God, they're gone. Thank you."

Rowan sat up. "Be careful, Vik. Yes, she's your sister, but something's wrong, and I can't shake the feeling you're in danger."

"All right. Eszter and this Niko person are meeting me at my parents' house tomorrow afternoon. Both my parents will be there."

"I have to go home. You'll be okay?"

"I'm more worried about you right now."

"I'll be fine." Rowan made Viktoria promise to call her with an update after the meeting, and the two women said their goodbyes.

After Rowan was gone, Viktoria realized she'd forgotten to mention the headstone image.

***

Maria and Antal Kovacs lived in a tidy bungalow in downtown Newmarket. Viktoria and Eszter had grown up in that house, walking distance to the shops and restaurants on Main Street South, the community centre, and Fairy Lake Park. Viktoria's apartment on Davis Drive was close enough for her to walk the few blocks, and she made sure she arrived two hours before Eszter and Niko were expected.

Viktoria sat in the armchair in the living room. Opposite her, her parents sat huddled together on the couch. Maria's eyes were red-rimmed but dry. Antal, grim and as pale as his olive skin would allow, stroked Maria's hair. His fingers fluttered through her grey-tinged black curls.

A sniffle escaped Maria, and she raised her eyes to meet Viktoria's concerned gaze.

"Eszter's back?" It was said in a whisper filled with hope and disbelief. "She's coming here?"

"Yes, Mamma," Viktoria whispered in response. Guilt had pricked her all night, chiding her for not calling them right away, but now she was glad she hadn't.

Her instincts had been right. They wouldn't have been able to sleep, would have stressed all night, anxious to see their child again. As it was, they could hardly stand waiting another hour until Eszter due to arrive.

They'd given Viktoria a difficult time when she'd first told them she'd seen Eszter and hadn't called the rest of the family to inform them of her return. Viktoria had spent most of the first hour since her arrival defending the decision.

Now, past the misplaced anger and struggling to accept the new reality, Maria and Antal stopped arguing.

"How was she?" Maria's thick, Hungarian accent made her sound brusque. "Did she seem okay? Was she hurt?"

"She looked fine. The man who rescued her, the one I told you she'll bring with her today, has been taking care of her." As Viktoria spoke, her gut clenched. Rowan's words of warning echoed in her ears.

Maria frowned. "Who is this man? Why didn't he bring her home before?"

Viktoria cleared her throat, buying some time. "Eszter didn't remember us. She said he found her wandering the streets." She sighed. The next words would be a struggle. Her parents hadn't reunited with their child yet—the child they'd believed might be dead—and Viktoria would have to tell them Eszter was dying.

"Mamma, Daddy." She paused, collected herself, and pushed ahead. "She looked fine, but she's not healthy. Eszter found out recently she has breast cancer. I'm sorry. She wanted me to prepare you before she gets here. It's terminal."

Maria leaped up. "No! What do you mean?" She rushed to where Viktoria sat. "Viki, why didn't you call me last night?"

"How would it have helped, Mamma. We went through this already." Viktoria rose and hugged her mother. "I'm sorry." She ran through everything Eszter had told her, including the refusal of alternative therapies.

"That's not my Eszter." Maria turned and stalked from the room.

Cupboard doors banged and dishes clattered in the kitchen.

"Viktoria!" Maria called out. "Help me fix up the snacks."

Snacks? Her mother couldn't have been knocked too far off centre if she was fiddling with food.

Viktoria walked to the kitchen.

Two large trays sat on the counter, and Maria was stacking homemade cookies from the freezer onto a plate.

When she spotted Viktoria, Maria waved a plump hand at her and said, "Make tea, please. And coffee. I don't know what Eszter likes now. Maybe she's so different." Her voice broke.

"Mamma." Viktoria hurried to her mother and gently put a hand on her shoulder. "We'll get through this. Whatever happens next, she returned to us. No more wondering. No more agonizing. We'll deal with anything else."

Part of her acknowledged the lie. Viktoria had spent most of the night before both wondering and agonizing. If only that nagging unease would leave her. Rowan's warnings hadn't helped either, but she refused to subject her parents to nebulous speculations.

Antal entered the room and went to the coffee maker. He opened the cupboard and retrieved the box of filters.

"I'll make the coffee, Viktoria. You make the tea." He glanced at Maria. "The cookies are nice. Eszter always loved them."

"Remember when she was nine and snuck into the basement to steal baking from the big freezer? She ate more than a dozen pastries before we caught her." Maria chuckled, but it sounded forced. "She made herself sick eating them frozen."

"Even ate the *Linzer* cookies," Antal said, "and she disliked those. Once, she even—"

"*Jaj, hol volt az a gyermek?*" Maria's voice broke loudly into Antal's musings.

"I don't know where she was, Mamma. All she told me was that Niko found her. Maybe she'll remember more as time goes on."

"What made her forget? That man? Who is he?" Maria returned to fiddling with the cookies.

"We'll find out. We'll listen to what they have to say, and we'll figure out what to do from there." Viktoria checked her watch, and her stomach fluttered. "They'll be here in five minutes."

Maria's hands froze over the platter. She glanced at Antal and then refocused on setting out the snacks.

Antal returned to making coffee, and Viktoria went to the water cooler to fill the kettle. As the minutes ticked by, the sense of foreboding she'd worked so hard to squelch returned.

CHAPTER 5

When Niko's car pulled into the driveway, all three Kovacses were standing at the living room's picture window watching for it. The teal green Porsche convertible pulled in behind Antal's red Toyota pickup truck, and the man who stepped from it made Viktoria's breath catch in her throat.

His black hair was curly and tousled, his lips full and sensual, reminding her of a young Jeff Goldblum. He wore a grey suit Viktoria assumed was expensive, and he wore it well. For a moment, Viktoria envied her sister this rugged, manly man.

He lifted his chin, and the cold steel in his eyes sent shudders through her. Was it anger? Callousness? Hatred? A jumble of toxic emotions flooded through her, and Viktoria had an urge to run outside and pull Eszter into the house where it was safe.

Next to Viktoria, Maria gasped, and when Viktoria glanced over, she caught her mother making the sign of the horns to ward off the evil eye.

While Maria had innate psychic abilities, she'd never developed them. She'd rejected them in her mother and denied them in her daughter. But during times of stress, her intuition asserted itself and leaked through despite her intentions to control it.

"He has blackness in him," Maria mumbled, and Viktoria had to strain to catch the words.

Viktoria didn't reply. She felt the same way.

Antal turned from the window and raced to the door. Before Niko and Eszter reached the front porch, Antal threw the door open and rushed down the steps to Eszter. He flung his arms around her, hugging her, kissing her cheek and her forehead. Tears streamed down his face.

For a moment, annoyance flashed across Eszter's face, but it came and went so quickly, Viktoria doubted she'd actually seen it. Then Eszter was embracing her father, sobbing in his arms, and kissing him back. "Daddy.

17

Oh, Daddy, I'm so sorry. I didn't know who I was."

"Okay, honey." Antal patted Eszter's back, reassuring her.

Maria gripped Viktoria's arm and said, "Watch that man."

Viktoria nodded. "Okay, Mamma."

Maria smiled then, her face an expression of sheer joy, and she rushed out of the house. "Eszter. Baby. My baby."

Eszter tore herself away from her father and hurled herself at her mother. "Mamma. Oh, Mamma. I'm home."

Viktoria stood in the doorway and studied Niko's reaction to the reunion. His gaze was levelled on Maria, and he wore a thoughtful expression. As if he sensed Viktoria's stare on him, he looked up and smiled. His eyes captivated; his face, unbearably handsome, made her breath catch once more. She could almost feel his arms around her and his lips on hers.

He stepped forward and broke the spell. Walking up to meet her, he held out his hand, and, involuntarily, she took it.

"You must be Viktoria." His voice was silk.

Viktoria caught a trace of an accent, reminding her of Khan in the original *Star Trek* show, and her heart raced.

Before she could speak, she had to clear her throat. "Yes. Nice to meet you."

His large hand continued to envelop hers, and his touch was cool and smooth. She imagined toxins flowing like sludge from his hand into hers. Alarmed, Viktoria tried to pull away, but he tightened his grip.

"So lovely. Like your sister." Slowly, as if it was his idea, he released her hand, which she snatched away and clasped behind her back.

"You're Niko," she said, needlessly. She refused to smile at him when alarm bells were clanging in the back of her brain. An image of Rowan flashed into her mind's eye, and it brought her peace. She exhaled, letting the tension out.

Movement in her periphery made her glance up. Her parents and sister headed up the front steps of the porch.

Eszter wore an enormous grin, and she gazed lovingly at Niko. "Everyone, I want you to meet Niko Farkas. He saved me. If it wasn't for Niko, I don't know where I'd be."

Maria narrowed her eyes as she turned from Eszter to Niko. "Hello. Come inside, please." She broke out into the lead and brushed past Niko with a nod, ignoring his extended hand.

He frowned, and Viktoria suspected he wasn't used to being dismissed. When Antal reached Niko, they clasped hands, but Antal reacted as Viktoria had: he tugged on the hand Niko held as though the contact repulsed him. Antal's eyes widened, and the two men locked gazes.

Niko smiled and released Antal's hand. "Nice to meet you, Mr.

Kovacs."

They shuffled into the living room, and Maria motioned for everyone to sit down. The cookies, coffee, and tea were spread out on the coffee table, along with milk and sugar.

"Please, help yourselves," Maria said.

Eszter slid onto the loveseat, pulling Niko down beside her, and grinned her appreciation. "Oh, pinwheels. And *Linzer* cookies. *Kifli*. Yummy. I feel like company." She snatched up a dessert plate and daintily set a few of the cookies on it. "Niko, try them. Mamma makes the best cookies. She used to make these when we were growing up. Right, Vik?"

Viktoria nodded as everyone turned to stare at her. "Yes, try them." The forced politeness grated on her nerves. Had Eszter lost her intuition when she'd disappeared? How could she sit next to this ... what? Viktoria couldn't put her finger on what she sensed from Niko. Was he a psychopath? If vampires existed, she'd consider the possibility.

Maybe that's it, she scoffed silently: he's a vampire.

"You're wondering about me, aren't you, dear sister?" Niko's voice was a low rumble.

Caught off guard, Viktoria felt her face flush. She dropped onto the couch and forced herself to meet his gaze. "You're a stranger. My sister has been missing for five years. She says you found her and kept her all that time." She nodded. "Yes, I'm wondering about you."

"Kept her. Did Eszter say that?" His lips curled into a humourless grin.

"N-no, not in those exact words." She glanced at Eszter, who'd lost her grin.

"Then tell us how you found Eszter and why you didn't bring her home when you did." Seated on the couch between his wife and Viktoria, Antal took Maria's hand.

Niko reclined in the loveseat, one arm draped along the back behind Eszter. "I found Eszter wandering around downtown Toronto. When I spotted her, I knew she was out of place. The area was wretched, filled with drug users and prostitutes. She didn't know who she was. Drugs she'd taken had made her incoherent." Niko paused and poured himself a cup of coffee. Everyone remained silent as he doctored it with sugar.

He glanced up, his gaze directed at Viktoria. "I like it black and sweet." He sipped and smiled. "Delicious. Where were we? Ah, yes. I didn't do anything for our poor Eszter then. I assumed she was one of the walking wounded you see downtown—homeless, neglected."

Maria sucked in a breath, and Niko turned his stare on her. "You're thinking that's cold—that I should have approached her then, yes?"

Maria opened her mouth, but it was Viktoria who spoke. "I'm wondering what you were doing there."

"Passing through. I own some buildings in the area and drive through sometimes." He squinted and continued the story. "I saw her and left her there, but I didn't forget her. Next time I cut through there, I spotted two lowlifes assaulting a young woman. When I recognized the lost soul I'd seen before, I intervened and brought her home."

"Where's home?" Antal asked.

"Outskirts of Newmarket." Niko raised his brows, flashed a smile. "I like my privacy and my space. Acreage. East on Davis Drive, past Woodbine Avenue."

"Then you'd have seen the posters we put up of Eszter when she went missing." Viktoria focused on pouring herself some tea and avoided his gaze.

"And heard the story in the news. I'm afraid I didn't make the connection. The photos I saw were of a clean, well-dressed college girl— not the street urchin I picked up."

"She cleans up good, though, doesn't she?" Viktoria stared at him.

He shrugged. "How could I have expected this to be the same young woman? Her hair in your photos was dark brown. The woman I found had the blonde hair you see now. I didn't make the connection."

"Even if she'd dyed it, the dark roots would have shown eventually."

At this, Eszter broke into the discussion. "Are you accusing him of something, Viki? It sounds as if you are."

"I'm trying to understand what happened." She turned back to Niko. "When exactly did you find Eszter?"

"I estimate two months after she disappeared. When I asked her who she was, she couldn't tell me. That quality that had kept her in my memory after the first time I saw her turned out to be an uncanny resemblance to my late wife. I started calling her Talitha."

"Why?" That was creepy and wrong. Viktoria tried to picture herself calling someone by a dead loved one's name and couldn't do it. "Smacks of unresolved issues, Niko, and makes me wonder what else you did with Eszter to recollect your late wife."

Eszter leaped up. "My God, Viktoria. That's nasty. We don't have to listen to this."

"Shh, Eszter." Maria stood and put a placating arm on Eszter's shoulder. "She doesn't mean it. We're worried, honey. We're afraid for you."

"Be afraid of my cancer, not of Niko." Her breath came in gasps. Posture rigid, her fists bunched at the end of stiffened arms. She spun on Viktoria and pointed an accusing finger at her. "I told you last night he saved me and that I didn't want him interrogated like a criminal."

Niko jumped to Eszter's side, and he folded her into his arms. "Darling, shh. I'm a big boy. I can take care of myself." He kissed the top of her head and stroked her hair with one hand.

Viktoria rose from her seat, and her parents followed her, so they all stood in a row between the coffee table and the couch.

"I'm sorry if I made you feel as though this is an interrogation, Niko." Viktoria had to force the polite tone, the fake regret. Deep inside remained the sense Niko was somehow responsible for Eszter's disappearance and, now, her reappearance.

He held his palm up at her and waved away the apology. "No need. I understand. Not knowing where your precious Eszter was must have terrified you. If I lost her now, I'd be devastated."

Eszter gazed up at him reverently. Her eyes shone with pleasure at his words.

Viktoria's gut clenched and an urge came over her to smack some sense into Eszter. "We need to notify the police—tell them she's home."

Immediately, Eszter's expression turned to one of horror. "I don't want to talk to the police."

"Why?" Viktoria jammed her fisted hands on her hips.

Again, Niko intervened. "They need to know, Tally." He flushed at the mistake. "I'm sorry. Habit. Eszter, we should report that you're home." He clasped her hands to his chest. "I'll be with you the whole time, my dear. It'll be okay."

"I'll be there, too," Viktoria said.

"We all will," Antal said. Before Eszter could protest, he went to the phone and dialled.

21

CHAPTER 6

Detective Clyde Baker had worked on Eszter's case since she'd disappeared. When Antal called to report Eszter's return, Baker immediately came out to the house.

He sat on an armchair across from Eszter, digital recorder on the coffee table and pen and notebook in hand. Everyone else clustered around him in their original seats. His gaze rarely left Eszter's face, even when someone else spoke, as Niko spoke now.

"She has been with me ever since, Detective. It wasn't until the shock of her cancer diagnosis and her memory returned that we learned she was the missing girl. In hindsight, I should have made the connection, but I didn't."

Baker glanced at Niko and then returned his gaze to Eszter. "Do you recall seeing Mr. Farkas before he took you to his home?"

"No. The first time I laid eyes on him was when he pulled those two men off me and took me off the streets." Eszter gazed worriedly at Niko as though confirming what she'd said met with his approval.

Niko nodded and gave her a comforting smile.

"It's hot out today, isn't it, Miss Kovacs?"

"Yes." Clearly, she was puzzled by Baker's question.

"Yet you're wearing long sleeves."

"I get chilled easily." She tossed a nervous glance at Niko.

"Are you right handed?"

"Yes."

"May I see your left arm, Miss Kovacs?" Baker leaned toward her and reached out his hands.

Eszter sucked in a breath. "Why?"

"May I?" He took her left hand, and when she tried to pull it away, he squeezed her fingers, maintaining the grip. "Don't worry." He pushed her sleeve up.

22

"But—"

Whatever she'd wanted to say was cut off by the collective gasp from Antal, Maria, and Viktoria. A long, white scar rode up the inside of Eszter's arm.

Eszter burst into tears, snatched her hand from Baker's grip, and buried her face in her palms. Sobs quivered her body.

Maria put an arm around Eszter. "Baby, what did you do? Oh, Eszter. My baby girl." Maria glared at Niko, who slid closer to Eszter and took her hands in his.

"Tell them what happened, sweetness." He leaned over and kissed her cheek, ignoring the hostile stares aimed at him.

Eszter nodded and sniffled. Maria handed her a tissue, and Eszter dabbed her eyes and wiped her nose.

"Mamma. I'm sorry." She folded herself into Niko's embrace. "Niko, you tell them. I hate to talk about it."

"Yes, honey. Okay." He kissed the top of her head and stroked her hair. When her breathing slowed, he stared at Baker and said, "She cut herself. It was shortly after I'd brought her to my home. Eszter's emotions were in turmoil."

Viktoria went to stand by the living room window. On the driveway across the street, a little boy pedalled back and forth on his tricycle while his mother dug in the flower garden. Niko's voice droned in Viktoria's ears.

"I didn't know what to do. She became more and more depressed. Nothing worked. I even got her a therapist."

"Why all that trouble for a complete stranger?" Viktoria didn't bother turning to face him. She didn't need to see his face to know this was all a lie, but how could she call him on it?

"I could afford it, and she didn't have anyone." He said it matter-of-factly, and Viktoria nodded. When he remained silent, she turned to face him.

"Why would I make this up, Viktoria? Eszter is right here to verify what I say."

She wouldn't contradict the man who controls her. The thought popped into her head and somehow felt right. Chills raced up Viktoria's spine.

"Okay." What else could she say? "Go on."

They continued to stare into each other's eyes. Just as she opened her mouth to tell him to continue, he spoke again.

"I thought the therapy was helping. She'd been with me for a month by then, and I had to return to work. My business will run without me for periods of time as long as I check in regularly, but I can't ignore it indefinitely."

He broke his eye-lock with Viktoria and spoke to Baker now. "She got hold of my razor blades. Thank God, I didn't leave her for long. I attended a breakfast meeting and popped back home to check on her. She was on the floor, bleeding out. I called nine-one-one and stopped the flow."

Niko patted his breast pocket, and Viktoria noted the outline of a cigarette pack in there. She smiled to herself. For the first time, he showed a sign of unease. She loved that he was jonesing for a smoke.

Eszter broke into sobs again, and Antal, Maria, and Niko crowded around her, offering hugs and reassurances.

Viktoria focused her gaze on Baker.

He leaned back in the armchair and observed the spectacle, occasionally adding something to his notes. His expression showed concern, but he didn't interfere or comment.

When Eszter was quiet again, Baker leaned forward once more and cleared his throat before he spoke. "I'm sorry you had such a difficult time, Miss Kovacs. Just another few minutes of your time, and we can close this case."

"Close it?" Viktoria burst out. "Why would you close it? We don't know who kidnapped her."

Baker swiveled his head around to meet her gaze. "Nothing back then indicated your sister had been kidnapped. Nothing here now changes my suspicion she was a runaway. She's not accusing anyone of kidnapping." He turned back to Eszter. "Correct, Miss Kovacs?"

"I guess," Eszter replied. "I don't remember leaving, and I only have a vague recollection of being on the streets." She shook her head. "No one forced me to leave, but I don't know why I did. I must have been depressed."

"You weren't depressed." The words spewed out in a burst of rage. Viktoria was close to shrieking. Over the last five years, she'd replayed the days before Eszter's disappearance so often, they were burned into her memory. "Detective, I told you then Eszter had no reason to run away." She threw his words back at him. "Nothing here now changes my suspicion she was coerced to leave."

"Then we'll have to agree to disagree once again, Miss Kovacs."

"You don't know Eszter like I do. She wouldn't have run away." Viktoria glared at Niko. "She wouldn't have tried to kill herself."

Eszter stood. "I want to go home, Niko. I can't listen to this anymore. Please." She pressed her palms together in front of her breasts as if in prayer. "Viki, Niko saved my life. Twice. We love each other. He's helping me deal with my illness. He brought me back to you."

Niko rose and put a hand on Eszter's shoulder. "I'll take you home. This has been an emotional few days for you. But your sister means well. She's only thinking of you, sweets." He put his arm around her. "Are you finished with her, Detective Baker?"

Viktoria gritted her teeth. What a phony. She glanced at her parents and

Baker. They were lapping it up. Maria's eyes shone with gratitude. How could that be? Didn't she sense the dark energy around Niko?

"You're free to go, Miss Kovacs. If I have any further questions, I'll be in touch."

"Thank you." Eszter shyly went to Viktoria and hugged her.

Viktoria returned the gesture and kissed Eszter on the cheek. "Call me if you need anything at all. Promise?" she whispered in Eszter's ear.

"I will. Thank you," Eszter replied.

As everyone said their goodbyes, Viktoria remained silent.

After Eszter, Niko, and Baker had left, Viktoria turned to her parents. "Don't you see there's something wrong with him?"

"I see she loves him," Maria said, "and he loves her."

"Mamma, don't you sense he's manipulating everyone? Why am I the only one to get that?" Frustrated, she paced the room. As she sailed past the coffee table, she absently snatched a pinwheel cookie from the plate and chewed on it. The vanilla and chocolate shortbread reminded her of her grandmother.

"You're suspicious, that's all." Antal stepped in her way, forcing her to stop walking. "We'll keep an eye on him. But if she's happy with him, why would we interfere?"

Maria picked up the tray of coffee and tea to take it to the kitchen. She paused at her husband's comment. "We don't have long with Eszter, so we have to make her last days comfortable and happy. Your father is right. If this man makes her happy, we won't do anything to keep them apart."

"What if he's the reason she's dying?" As soon as she said it, Viktoria knew it wasn't true. The image of the grave with Eszter's name on it popped into her head again. She still didn't know what it meant, but to help Eszter, she'd have to figure it out.

CHAPTER 7

Errands and work on the spare bedroom she'd started redecorating the previous weekend consumed the remainder of Viktoria's time off from the store. She was grateful for the distraction of doing the second coat of paint and ordering new carpeting and furniture. But it never took her mind completely off her sister. She texted Rowan that all was well but didn't call her.

On Monday night, Viktoria did another reading for herself, once again getting confusing results. She tried to focus on the outcome for her sister's treatment, and again got the grave with date of Eszter's death marked as shortly after the day she disappeared.

When she returned to work on Tuesday, she greeted Rowan's cheery "good morning" with a frustrated "what's good about it?" Immediately, she regretted the sniping.

"I'm sorry, Ro. I haven't had my caffeine fix yet."

"That's okay." Rowan's smile held concern. "You look tired. There's a pot of tea in the back."

Viktoria strode to the back room and put her purse in the cupboard. She went in the kitchen, poured herself a mug of tea from the cozied pot, and took it out to the front. According to the schedule, her first reading wouldn't be for another hour, and there were no customers in the store yet. Relieved, she set the mug on the counter and hugged Rowan.

"Oh, Ro, it's been so difficult."

"All right, honey. Why didn't you call me? I'd have come over."

Viktoria squelched the tears that threatened and released Rowan from the death grip.

"I kept myself busy so I wouldn't think about it. Besides, I didn't want to dump on you." She sighed and then inhaled deeply, letting the scent of mastic and sage permeating the room calm her.

"You're not dumping on me. What happened when you met with Eszter at your parents' place?"

Viktoria told Rowan all about it and insisted something was preventing her parents from seeing Niko as he truly was.

"Why wouldn't you be blocked too, then?" Rowan asked. She held up a hand, palm out, as Viktoria opened her mouth to reply. "I'm not implying they're right and you're imagining things."

"Then what are you saying?"

"I'm wondering if you're picking up something from the past and not the present. Maybe getting some mixed signals or misinterpreting. If someone wanted to block that information, wouldn't it make sense they'd block you? You're the one who's a psychic and closest to Eszter. You're twins, for crying out loud."

The moment Rowan stopped speaking, both women stared at each other. A chill made Viktoria shiver, and Rowan hugged herself as goose bumps prickled her arms.

"Twins," Rowan said. "Tough to sever that connection."

"I was blocked when she disappeared. It was pathetic how impotent I was."

"Could be there was more of a focus on obstructing you then, or perhaps now Eszter's back in your life, it's harder to impede what she'd send you willingly."

"Yes. If any of what they said happened, she would've been confused, and it would've been easier to block energy links between us. But why would someone go to all that trouble?"

The bell on the door jingled, and the conversation had to be tabled to serve customers. Time slid by as more people arrived, and when Viktoria caught her breath, it was almost ten o'clock.

"If this Aedan McCarthy guy doesn't show up soon, he'll be late for his reading." Viktoria commented. "I've never seen his name on the schedule before. Someone you know?"

Rowan shrugged. "He phoned to schedule it, and when I booked him in, I had to give him directions to the store, too. Says he heard about the place from a friend, but when he mentioned a name, I didn't recognize it."

Viktoria shrugged. "I guess we'll find out more when he gets here. If he gets here. Maybe he changed his mind."

No sooner had she said that than the bells clattered, and a man walked into the store.

Sexy was Viktoria's first thought. Something familiar about him was her second. He wore jeans and a pale blue shirt, open at the neck. The sleeves were rolled up, and his wavy brown hair brushed the top of his collar at the back. He reminded her of a young Han Solo, and that wasn't hard to take at all.

Focus, Viktoria. His hotness had better not stymie her psychic abilities.

"Hi, ladies. I'm here to see Viktoria Kovacs." His voice was a smooth baritone that sent a shiver through her, as if she'd just been stroked by a feather. This next hour would be a long one if she'd have to check her libido at the reading room entrance.

"That's me." Her voice came out breathy, and a flush crept over her face. *Oh, God.* She shook it off and stepped from behind the counter, holding her right hand out for him to shake. "You must be Aedan McCarthy. Have we met before?"

He clasped her hand and gave it a firm pump before releasing it. "No, I doubt it. I'd remember you after one look."

Viktoria chewed on her lip to prevent herself from giggling like a schoolgirl. "Come on back to the reading room."

She glanced at the clock—still a few minutes to spare, so she wouldn't have to read him the punctuality riot act. Without verifying that he followed her, she headed through the bead curtains into the back of the store. She continued through the room they used for workshops and hooked a left into the reading room.

The audible inhale behind her made her turn around to see what of the many strange and ornate trinkets accenting the room had caught his eye. The way his head swiveled, left, right, up, and down, made her conclude they all had.

Amused, she studied him as he sidestepped to an enormous Buddha meditating atop a waterfall flowing into a lotus-blossom-covered pond. The remnants of this morning's saging session spiced up the room, and like a dog catching a scent, Aedan sniffed the air. "Is that what I think it is?"

She smiled. "If you think it's sage, then yes, it's what you think it is."

He chuckled. "Okay. Sure."

She caught the sparkle in his deep, brown eyes, and her smile turned into a grin.

Viktoria waved him to a chair, took the seat across from his, and waited for him to settle. In the meantime, she picked up a deck of angel cards. After a moment, she switched them out for fairy cards. The mischief energy of the fairies suited him, and the Irish McCarthy name made her think the fairies would enjoy getting involved in this reading.

"Have you had a reading before?" She shuffled the cards as she talked, clearing them, infusing them with her energy.

"No."

"What inspired you to make this appointment?"

He hesitated, and she got an image flash of a computer keyboard.

"You work on the computer?"

"Yes." He raised his brows in surprise.

Strange. What would that have to do with him booking a reading? She

28

shrugged it off. She'd wait and see. The answer would come eventually.

"So, why this appointment?" She almost asked if there was something specific he needed to discuss but stopped herself. His response was important. She didn't know why, but he had to answer the question, and she had to be careful not to lead him.

Silently, she asked for clarification. Was he a computer programmer? An electronics engineer? A pen flashed into her head. Ah, a writer. Viktoria waited in silence. No need to let on just yet she was downloading information.

"My friend suggested I book a reading here when I told him I was interested in getting one."

"Yes, that's what you told Rowan."

But there was more.

What's black and white and read all over? The old joke popped into her head, and suddenly she knew. Anger made her leap up from her chair, knocking it over as she dropped the cards and lurched backward.

"How dare you?" she said. "Did you think I wouldn't intuit why you're here? I'm not doing this. Get out, and I doubt Rowan will allow you to ever return."

CHAPTER 8

"Whoa, wait a minute." Aedan leaped up, his expression confused. "What's wrong? What did I do?"

"You came here as a journalist, not as a client. If you want to write about me or what I do, the least you could do is ask me if I mind."

"It's not like that." He walked around to her side of the table and righted her chair. "Sit. Let's discuss this rationally."

When she made no move to do as he asked, he held the back of the chair and executed a slight bow. "Please. If you're still mad at me, I'll leave. But I'd like my hour, and I assure you, I won't do a news story about you."

Warily, she sat. "But you're a journalist?"

"Yes. Did you recognize me from my column? The picture's a little outdated." He returned to his seat.

"No. I don't know why you seemed familiar. What column do you write? I can't place you."

"How flattering." But he smiled. "I write crime stories. Mostly investigative follow-ups and feature stories. I freelance and write a regular column for the *York Region Gazette*."

"Why are you here? What are you writing about that you need to investigate me? And why didn't you tell me about it?"

He sighed and ran a hand through his hair. "I'm working on a novel. This is research. I planned to tell you after the reading. The only reason I didn't tell you upfront was that I wanted an honest reading, without bias. I was afraid if you knew I was writing a novel, it would influence you."

Her eyes narrowed, and she scowled. "Why you—"

"Whoa, don't jump to more conclusions." He folded his hands in front of him on the table and waited. "You calm?"

She nodded, but inside, she seethed. How dare he come here to test her? And then accuse her of dishonesty when he didn't even know her? She bit her lip to keep from shouting at him.

"I'm not implying you wouldn't intend to give me an honest reading. But I'm a skeptic—an open-minded one, I like to think—but a skeptic. Look, I have no idea how this works. Telling you I'm researching a novel might affect your abilities. It might influence you, even unconsciously, and I wanted to avoid that. I was being logical."

"Implying I'm emotional?" Why were the hot guys always jerks?

"Aren't you?"

Her jaw dropped. He had here there. She'd jumped first to the conclusion he would do a smear piece on her and second that he wanted to trip her up. It wouldn't have been the first time someone had tried to mess with her, and it never went well for either side.

"You're right." She leaned back in her chair, anger defused. "I've had my fill of debunkers, Mr. McCarthy. I don't mind skeptics, but those who expect me to perform for them so they can humiliate me and waste my time burn me up."

"And you thought that's what I was doing?"

"I guess we both made some incorrect assumptions. Would you like to start over?" She glanced at the time. "I can still give you your full hour. I always leave a half hour between readings, just in case. We have time."

"All right." He sat up straight. "Are you okay to do this? Did this"—he waved his hands in the air—"outburst throw you off?"

"I'm fine." She picked up the fairy deck again. Mischief indeed. She'd called it correctly. "This session might be for research, but the reading is for you. Anything specific you want to explore? Health? Finances? Relationship? Career?" When she said relationship, her stomach fluttered.

She took a deep breath and cleared herself. *Not now, Viktoria. Focus on service.*

"What do you suggest?"

"If you aren't sure, I can do a general reading. We'll ask the fairies to tell us what they want you to know."

He didn't bat an eye at the mention of fairies—she gave him points for that.

"All right. A general reading, then." She shuffled, focusing on Aedan McCarthy and what he should know. "The cards work on the Law of Attraction. Are you familiar with it?"

He shook his head.

"Like attracts like. You attract what you think about most. The cards I pull will reflect what's happening in your life right now. If you'd have asked a specific question, the cards would echo that. It'll reflect whatever your focus is." She stopped shuffling and dealt out three cards, face up and directed at Aedan.

"You're concerned about your career. All three cards show that." She pointed to the first one, a fairy astride a rearing horse. The caption underneath read "It's okay to release the reins."

"This one tells you to let go of your need to control everything." An image flashed into her head. "Rules at the office make you feel trapped and controlled. Politics get under your skin."

She sensed Aedan nodding but ignored it. Her focus was down and to the right so the images would continue to come in. "You prefer to work at home, not at the office, because you need autonomy and control. Did you recently have a change in your schedule?" She didn't wait for a reply. "You feel restricted and need to make changes in the amount of time you spend at the office."

Viktoria finally met his gaze.

He shrugged. "Okay."

She examined the next card, a fairy spiraling in a vortex. The caption read "Help is on the way."

Viktoria focused again, down and to the right.

"An unhealthy situation is brewing. Your desire to help will drag you into something unpleasant. There's that control factor again." An image of a shark flashed into her head. A symbol.

"Someone predatory. Cold. He's—"

Niko. She gasped.

"What is it?" Aedan frowned.

"Be careful who you trust." Could he possibly know Niko? "Have you ever met a man named Nikolas Farkas?"

"Yes. His company owns the newspaper's office building. I've met him on a number of occasions. I've interviewed him more than once and have run into him at social events. Why?"

Her hands shook, so she clasped them in her lap. "I'm sorry. We have to stop this reading."

"Why? What did I do?"

"It's not you." She willed the trembling from her hands and failed. She gathered up her cards. "It's getting too personal."

"I don't understand, Miss Kovacs."

Carefully, she placed the deck back in its box and closed the lid. The fairy child on the box gazed back at her, its gossamer wings glittering. "I'm seeing images of someone I know. I've got a conflict of interest here. I'm sorry. Obviously, I won't charge you for this."

***

When Viktoria mentioned Niko Farkas, Aedan was shocked but not as shocked as he was when she declared she couldn't finish his reading. "Why is this a conflict of interest? You read for friends and family, don't you?"

"It's not that simple. When I read for a friend, I don't accept money for it. You can't be my client. My sister is involved with Niko Farkas."

Aedan tried to supress the rising irritation. Was she serious? Or was she doing this out of spite because she thought he'd tried to mess with her. "I'm not messing with you."

Suddenly, it was too much for him. He stood up. "Fine. I'll reschedule with someone else." He glared down at her. "All I wanted was a psychic reading. That's it. The experience of it. And then maybe a discussion about the process. But if that's too difficult for you, then hey, I'll find someone else."

As his rant wound down, he realized her eyes were wide with fear, her face had drained of colour, and her hands shook.

God, he didn't want to get involved, but she looked so vulnerable. "What is it you're afraid of?"

She stood. "I'm fine. You need to go."

"What's wrong with Farkas? What did you see that concerns me?" His hands curled into fists on his hips. The least she could do was tell him if she saw this guy burning him in some way.

She gave an audible sigh. "Do you believe in fate?"

"Are we going to have a philosophical discussion so you don't have to answer my question?"

"There's a point to this. Do you?"

"No. We make our own fate."

"Terrific. Then there's nothing to worry about. He'll only be a problem for you if you get entangled in his business. You said you barely know him, right?"

"Right."

"Then stay out of his business." She hesitated. "That includes anything to do with me."

He studied her. She was attractive, no doubt about it. When he'd first set eyes on her, his body had reacted. When he'd shook her hand, he'd felt a spark. Maybe it was those gypsy eyes; the lush, smooth hair that made him want to run his fingers through it and grip it in his fist; or maybe the long legs that he could envision parting just for him.

The room grew hot, and sweat dewed his back.

Jesus, if he didn't rein in these thoughts, he'd throw her down on the reading room table and get entangled with her right there. What the fuck was wrong with him?

Aedan scrubbed his hands over his face and forced his breathing to slow. "You're saying I can't associate with you because your sister is dating Niko Farkas, a man I hardly know?"

Viktoria gave a slight nod. "Sounds crazy, but you don't understand."

"Then enlighten me."

"What does it matter?" A frown replaced the shock and fear on her face.

Mission accomplished. Better she find him irritating rather than frightening, though he suspected it wasn't him who'd scared her. "So, if I don't stay away from you, I'm fated to have trouble from Farkas?"

"Yes."

"Why? What's it to him?"

She averted her eyes. "That's what I can't discuss with you."

"Okay. Fine." He offered her his hand, and she rose to her feet and took it.

Ignoring how the soft, warm touch speared electricity through him, Aedan shook her hand. Before he released it, he had a strong desire to draw her into his arms. Instead, he let her go.

"Nice meeting you. Have a good life." The irritation in his voice shocked him, but he refused to apologize for it. If that's how she wanted it, then that's how it would be. They'd just met for Christ's sake. He could walk out and forget about her. They meant nothing to each other. Why were all the hot chicks crazy?

"Nice meeting you, too." She sank back into her seat, picked up her card deck, and started shuffling the cards.

When he glanced back as he closed the door behind him, she was laying them out in front of her.

CHAPTER 9

The room felt empty without his presence, and Viktoria berated herself when the urge to chase him down hit her. She had to let him go. If he got involved with her, even in a reader-client relationship, he'd suffer for it—she'd seen that in the images that had poured in when she viewed the second card in his reading.

Niko Farkas was a dangerous man. She was certain of it now but no nearer to proving it. Everything she had was based on intuition.

The door opened and Rowan entered.

"What happened, Viki? He didn't stay long enough to get a reading, didn't pay me as he left—hell, he barely spoke to me. All he did was say he had to reschedule, wave goodbye at me, and stalk out like hellhounds were chasing him."

"I asked him to leave. Did you know he's a journalist?"

"He didn't tell me that, no. But we don't discriminate here. It doesn't matter what he does for a living. I know it's not his profession that bothers you. What did he do to piss you off?"

"I'm not mad at him—well, not now, anyway. He really did want a reading. He's doing research for a novel. We cleared the air about how he should be more upfront about approaching psychics for research. I'm sure he meant it when he said he wasn't a debunker."

"But?"

She sighed. "Damn it, Rowan. He knows Niko Farkas, and if Aedan McCarthy gets sucked into my life, which apparently he would if I keep doing readings for him, he'll have trouble. I won't be responsible for that."

"Why would it be your responsibility?"

"My fault, then."

"What's your fault?"

Viktoria eyed the cards she'd laid out. The card representing emotional

35

healing was first, a love life card was second, and a power card was third. Did her emotions need healing? She supposed they did. Eszter's disappearance had disrupted Viktoria's life, her emotional state—everything about her. All levels of her being had been affected.

"Viki." Rowan's voice brought her out of her reverie.

"I'm trying to get myself sorted out, Ro." She rested her elbows on the table and buried her face in her palms. "If Aedan got yanked into my life, he'd get on Niko Farkas's radar, and any resulting trouble would be my fault. I have to push him away."

Rowan sat down.

Viktoria raised her head. "Who's minding the store?" Viktoria was grateful for Rowan's company, but her friend had a business to run.

"Don't worry. Mackenzie's here. I asked her to take the cash while I checked on you." Rowan's daughter, Mackenzie, often helped out at the store behind the cash register though her main focus was creating crafts and giftware to sell.

"Okay." Viktoria pointed to the second card. "My love life is looking up, apparently. I'm attracted to him, and we have a connection even if most of our time together this morning was spent arguing. Why does it have to be this way? Why does my intuition tell me we'd be great together and yet tell me to reject him?"

"He came into your life for a reason. It's not up to you to force anything or struggle against it. Whether or not he wants to get involved in your crazy life should be his decision. Has he indicated any interest in you that way?"

Viktoria laughed. "No. But I could sense the desire." She swiped the cards back into the pile while she reflected on the third card: Power. Her power. If she interpreted it correctly, she'd need to build her witch powers to get through what was coming. She'd seen darkness, but she'd also seen light shining through it.

"Foresight isn't a gift. It's a curse. People come to us to learn their future. They want the mystery removed, to hear everything will be all right."

"Yes, they do." Rowan picked up a deck of cards and shuffled.

"They assume if they predict misfortune, they'll avoid it."

"That's the hope."

"Yeah, but it doesn't always work out. Sometimes you're supposed to go through the bad time—and damn it, that's what you're telling me."

"And sometimes you can prevent it."

"That's part of my struggle. What many don't realize is most future events aren't meant to be seen. Besides, if you take free will out of the equation, you won't be happy no matter what the outcome. You're like a leaf blowing in the wind then." Viktoria's voice had grown loud with passion.

"Maybe they like someone else pulling their strings. Some people don't want control. Others want to control everything. That's your issue, sweetie."

"I'm not a control freak."

Rowan sputtered. "What? Now who do you think you're talking to?"

"I'll give you that I like being in charge of my life. But I don't try to control anyone else's life."

"You're doing it now." Rowan said it matter-of-factly as she dealt three cards, changed her mind, and laid out the Celtic cross.

"No, I'm not."

"What do you think you were doing when you told Aedan to leave and have nothing more to do with you? What makes you believe it's not in your best interests to have a relationship—and by 'your' I mean you and Aedan."

"Growth through suffering? Uh-uh. I'm not buying it."

"What makes you conclude you'll be suffering? And by 'you' I mean—"

"Yeah, you mean me and him. Ro, I saw the suffering. The cards were lousy with it. So were the messages I got. It'll get dangerous, and I refuse to drag a man into that. I'd rather die, and I mean that literally."

Frowning, eyes troubled, Rowan waved her hand over the card spread. She scooped them back up and returned them to the box. "Things will work out the way they're meant to." She rose abruptly.

"You always say that."

"Because it's true." She started to leave but turned back to face Viktoria when she reached the door. Rowan's serious expression softened into a smile. "Now you have a free hour, come out front and help me price and shelve the new stock. It'll take your mind off your troubles."

Viktoria smiled. "Sure."

After Rowan left, Viktoria eyed the card deck her friend had left behind. The reading had scared Rowan. Viktoria considered opening the box and reviewing the cards. They'd be sitting in order—she'd watched Rowan put them away. But that would be invading Rowan's privacy. Better to ask Rowan to tell her what she'd seen.

What if Rowan had seen a warning about Niko, about him harming Rowan, her daughter, or the store? She'd be one more person associated with Viktoria who had misfortune in her future.

Viktoria didn't believe in coincidences. Eszter had come back, bringing Niko Farkas with her, and suddenly the future appeared bleak for anyone connected to the Kovacs family.

"Viki?" Rowan stood at the door. "What's happening?" She sucked in a breath when she noticed where Viktoria's focus was. "Never mind the cards."

"Tell me what you saw. You have to, so we can deal with it together," Viktoria said.

"It's personal. We don't have to deal with it. I do."

"Are you saying it had nothing to do with me?"

Rowan shook her head. "Not everything is about you, Viktoria."

"I'm not so self-absorbed to think it is, but I'm afraid. So promise me whatever you saw in those cards didn't involve me and my family."

"It didn't. Come on. I've had enough of this doom and gloom for one morning." Rowan turned and walked away.

Viktoria followed Rowan into the store. But the unease remained. Somehow, whatever Rowan had seen would relate back to Niko, and if it did, then it involved Viktoria and her family. She'd have to find a way to learn what Rowan didn't want to reveal.

CHAPTER 10

At his home in Newmarket, Aedan McCarthy sat at his computer and forced himself to focus on his research. He bookmarked another new age store's website that had possibilities. The "Contact Us" page showed its location as a plaza at Mulock Drive and Yonge Street, which was near the Stonehaven subdivision where Aedan lived.

He had a reading booked in the afternoon with a woman who claimed to communicate with animals. Aedan glanced at Puddles, his border collie. The dog had outgrown the bad habit of watering the hardwood that had earned him his name. Still, Aedan was relieved he wouldn't have to take the dog with him when he went to see the woman. She'd told him all she needed was a photo.

His thoughts wandered back to his dust-up with Viktoria. At first, he'd considered avoiding The Green Witch all together. She didn't want him in her life? Fine. They just lost a client. But after he'd cooled off, he'd called the store and booked a reading with Angela, one of the other readers. She had a good reputation, and Rowan recommended her highly.

As Rowan discussed dates and times with him, Aedan had the urge to ask when Viktoria would be there so he could avoid her. Again he reconsidered. She meant nothing to him. If he bumped into her when he went for his reading, she'd have to deal with it. He refused to let her dictate where he could go and when he could go there.

He'd even asked Rowan if he could hang out at the store and observe their day-to-day activities as part of his research. To his surprise, Rowan had agreed. Either Viktoria hadn't told Rowan what had happened between them, or she was attempting to stay neutral.

Part of him gleefully anticipated Viktoria's reaction when he showed up there. Another part of him just wanted to see her again.

And that pissed him off.

She'd gotten under his skin and into his head.

As he clicked through the results list on his search for other new age stores, he grumbled. "She dresses like a hippie, Pud. Some flowy tie-dyed blouse and flouncy skirt. Hides her legs, but I can tell she's got a pair under all that." He shot a glance at Puddles.

The dog stared back silently, his nose on his paws.

"Can you believe she kicked me out?"

After a moment, Aedan nodded his head as though the dog had scored a point. "Yeah, you're right. I should have told her upfront I'm doing research. Lesson learned. I did that with all the other readings I booked. But pal, she was okay with it. She started to do the reading, and then bam!" He clapped his hands, and Puddles jumped up.

"Okay, boy. Sorry. But she had no cause. I only know Niko Farkas in passing. If he saw me on the street, he wouldn't recognize me. So he owns the office's building. So what? That doesn't make us buddies. He wouldn't invite me to his wedding or his stag—though I'd bet that would be a blast."

Aedan opened another tab on his browser. "Maybe I should do a little research on him, find out what the hell has Viktoria Kovacs's hippie skirt in a knot."

He entered "Nikolas Farkas" into the search box and hit enter.

A long list of results returned, the top one linking to a current news story—dated with yesterday's date. And it mentioned the name "Kovacs."

Aedan clicked on it and leaned in to read.

The headline read *Missing Coed Found with Magnate Nikolas Farkas*. As Aedan read through the article, he grew increasingly suspicious of the story.

Farkas claimed he'd found the girl in a seedy part of downtown Toronto and had rescued her from an assault in progress. Conveniently, she had no recollection of how she'd gotten to Toronto, and neither of them had connected her to the missing woman from Newmarket.

Were they both involved in her disappearance, or was one of them being conned? Maybe the woman was scamming Farkas for his money. He rescued her from the streets, and she was cashing in on a good thing. Interesting that they'd never reported the assault.

Eszter Kovacs. Viktoria's sister. Viktoria had said Farkas was dating her sister.

Aedan glanced at the dog again. "She was afraid. When she told me to leave, she was scared spitless." He checked the time. He'd been sitting for more than an hour. Time to take a break. Aedan stood, stretched, and went to the kitchen to put on coffee.

He wouldn't have to go out for another few hours. In the meantime, he would do a little digging and find out what Eszter Kovacs and Niko Farkas were up to. College girl disappears for five years and turns up living with a millionaire—it would make an interesting story. If the paper didn't want it, he could sell it to a magazine.

As the coffee maker rumbled to completion and the aroma of fresh brew wafted into the air, Aedan planned strategy. The realization dawned that he'd have to interview Viktoria. Based on this morning's events, she wouldn't cooperate. Maybe he could figure out a way to charm and disarm her.

Yeah, right. After the row they'd had this morning, subterfuge wouldn't be the way to get an interview. What if he reasoned with her? Told her he wanted to get the truth out there, stop the rumours? Somehow, he doubted she'd go for that.

Fuck it.

He'd take the direct approach, and if she refused to comment, he'd do what he always did in that situation: work around it. In the end, he could write the story without her cooperation. Hell, he could write it without talking to her at all. He'd already spent some time with her, and she'd warned him about Farkas.

What had she said?

Forgetting about his coffee, Aedan rushed back to his computer and created a new file for the Eszter Kovacs disappearance article. He'd write down whatever he remembered from his brief session with Viktoria. With some effort, he could get a quote from her out of it without even speaking to her again. Whether or not Viktoria wanted it, Aedan McCarthy was involved in her life.

He chuckled. Maybe it was fate.

***

Viktoria had known it was Aedan McCarthy on the phone by the way Rowan's gaze darted to Viktoria and then away again. She didn't try to listen in on the conversation, but she didn't give Rowan privacy either. It was a store phone at a cash register. Lack of privacy was a given.

When Rowan hung up, Viktoria kept her gaze down and forced herself to continue stocking shelves.

"He's seeing Angela."

Without looking up, Viktoria said, "Who?"

"I know you were listening, and you know who called. I also know you're curious, so I'm telling you even though you haven't asked."

She sighed. "Okay, fine. I'm curious."

"He didn't mention you."

"Why would I care about that? And why would he?"

"Because you threw him out of here. It makes me a little suspicious."

She raised her head. "Why?"

"Anyone else in that situation would have asked about you. Most people wouldn't have been content to let it rest, and you said he's a reporter?"

"Journalist."

"Same thing."

"It's not, but I understand what you mean. Well, when he comes in for his reading, Angela can deal with him."

"Good, because he's coming in tomorrow morning, and I told him he could hang out here."

Viktoria's head snapped up.

"Research. I don't mind helping him out. He's got good energy, and it'll be exposure for the store."

Viktoria shrugged. "He hasn't offended me. It's okay for him to be here—he just can't form a relationship with me."

Rowan laughed. "I wasn't implying you have a crush on him." She grew serious then. "You don't have to explain anymore. If you want to avoid him, take your lunch when he shows up, as long as you don't mind waiting until one to go. But if he hangs out here, you'll have to tolerate him."

"Sure. I'll be fine." She'd be polite. It wasn't necessary to avoid him. All she needed to do was keep her distance.

The phone rang again and Rowan picked up. "Green Witch."

The bell above the door jingled, and Viktoria smiled as she turned to face whoever had entered the store. Her heart thudded against her chest when she recognized Eszter and Niko. She gripped the edge of the counter until her knuckles whitened.

"Eszter. Niko. What are you doing here?"

Rowan put protection spells around the store. Shouldn't that have kept Niko out?

"We were in the neighbourhood. Niko's company is building a subdivision around here. He wanted to show me how it was coming along, and we thought we'd check out where you work while we're at it."

Okay, you've seen it. Now, get out. She kept that to herself, but boy, would she have loved to say it out loud. A shudder rocked her, and she drew her shawl tight around her body to ward off the sudden chill in the room.

Unable to move or speak, Viktoria's gaze followed the pair as they walked around the store, checking out the merchandise.

Eszter appeared delighted as she poked around in the crystals and peered at the various figurines in the display case.

Niko arched a brow at Rowan when she set down the phone and met his gaze.

"Ms. Swift. How nice to make your acquaintance. I'm Nikolas Farkas."

Rowan's expression remained impassive. "What can I do for you today, Mr. Farkas?"

"Please, call me Niko. We'll be neighbours soon, and I wanted to check out the local colour. Your little shop is enchanting."

Rowan's stance and expression didn't change, but she paled at his words. Voice even, she said, "You're moving to Sharon?"

"Yes." He picked up an intricately carved bronze figure of Archangel Michael slaying the serpent. "Sharon will provide me with what I need." He set the figure back on the shelf, his motions gentle, careful.

"What might that be?"

Viktoria admired Rowan for having the balls to question Niko, but they were on her turf, and Rowan was a powerful witch. He didn't intimidate her, though Viktoria could tell her friend had been rattled by Niko's presence.

"Suburbs with a country feel. Proximity to your lovely store." He smirked as he said it, and Viktoria shuddered again.

A heaviness pervaded her limbs, and she gulped air as if finding oxygen in short supply.

Rowan's eyes narrowed when her gaze snapped onto Viktoria. "Viki, do me a favour and check if the kettle has boiled."

Viktoria nodded and shuffled out from behind the counter. As she made her way to the back, she sneaked a glance at Niko.

A single bead of sweat ran down his temple, and he held his jaw clenched tight.

CHAPTER 11

In the back room, Viktoria waited for her breathing to return to normal. She remained hidden near the bead curtain. The kettle was fine. They hadn't plugged it in yet today. *I have to get back in there. Rowan's alone with them.*

Viktoria was grateful for the reprieve and the chance to collect herself, but she refused to hide like a coward. Rowan was holding her own, but how long would that last? Why didn't they leave?

Eszter probably wouldn't leave without saying goodbye to her sister, so Viktoria fisted her hands, took a deep breath, and stepped into the room.

"Kettle's fine, Ro." Viktoria scanned the store.

Niko had moved to the perimeter of the room, near the exit. Eszter stood before a display of herbs and spell candles in various colours. She picked through the four-inch tapers.

"Eszter." Niko's voice was terse.

Eszter startled and dropped the item in her hands. She frowned. "Yes?"

"We need to go, my love." His hands, too, were balled into fists, the knuckles white.

Tension releasing, Viktoria opened her hands and flexed her fingers.

Niko tapped his foot, obviously impatient to leave. The air around him shimmered, thick and heavy. He checked the watch on his wrist.

Eszter walked to the counter. "Let's get together for dinner tomorrow night, okay?" she said to Viktoria.

The last thing she wanted to do was have dinner with Niko.

As if reading her mind, Eszter said, "Just you and me. We'll meet at the pub on Main Street—the one with the patio in the back."

"Okay." If she agreed, they'd leave faster. All she wanted right now was to get them out of the store. "Six?"

"Sure. I'll see you then." Eszter turned to Rowan. "Nice meeting you."

"You too," Rowan replied.

44

"Come along, Eszter. We're out of time." Niko turned his gaze from Viktoria to Rowan. "Very nice store you have here, Ms. Swift. I'll be sure to visit often. Have a good day."

He pulled open the door, jingling the bell, and guided Eszter outside with his hand on the small of her back.

The moment the door closed behind them, Rowan raced over, locked it, and turned the "Open" sign to "Closed." She set the "Back in X Minutes" message to twenty.

"Thank the Goddess, they're gone. I need to recover." Rowan strode to the bead curtain and paused. "I'll make tea. Come on back."

"I'm sorry, Ro." Viktoria followed Rowan into the kitchen and leaned against the fridge while Rowan filled the kettle.

"Why? What did you do?"

"They wouldn't have come here if it wasn't for me."

"I wouldn't be so sure." Rowan set the kettle on the base and pressed the on switch. She leaned against the counter by the sink. "He came to check me out and used your relationship as an excuse."

"Now who thinks everything is about them?" Viktoria grinned to show she was kidding. She glanced down and to the right, trying to focus on receiving information about the encounter.

"Oh, my God." She gaped at Rowan. "He did. Why? And, more important, how did he get past your protection spells?"

"I hate to admit it, but he's powerful—maybe more than me. He dabbles deep into dark magick, so he'll do anything to get what he wants." She dropped a couple of tea bags into the teapot. "The protections I put up are designed to keep toxic energy out, but anyone powerful enough can get through it. It takes energy to maintain it."

Sweat had gleamed at Niko's temple and his body had tensed. He'd practically hurled himself out the door when he'd left.

"He felt it. That's why they left so abruptly, isn't it?" Viktoria said.

Rowan nodded. "He could only fight the energy here for so long before it repelled him. I may not have been able to keep him out, but he couldn't tolerate it forever."

The kettle clicked off, and Rowan poured the water into the teapot. "I'm happy to see it worked, but I'll also have to expend extra energy on fortifying it." She sighed. "I don't expect it'll keep him out though. Did you hear how he said he'd be back?"

"Yes."

"He's arrogant. He wanted me to know he was aware of the protection spells but would come and go as he pleases. The son of a bitch was taunting me."

"My sister thinks he's Mr. Wonderful. Can we do a spell?"

"You know the answer to that."

45

She did. The threefold law: whatever you put out there would come back to you threefold. And the Wiccan Rede: An' it harm none, do as ye will. Oh, she wanted to harm all right. "Niko doesn't abide by them."

"Niko's ego makes him believe he'll get away with it."

"I don't see him being punished."

Rowan poured the tea. "He might be." She doctored the teas and handed Viktoria the one with sugar and milk. "We have to protect ourselves against him, but we shouldn't cause him harm."

"I want to get Eszter away from him. He's using her."

"Then do it the old-fashioned way."

When Viktoria shot Rowan a puzzled look, Rowan laughed. "Talk to her."

Viktoria grinned. "I guess I could give that a shot." Suddenly, she wanted to have that dinner with Eszter.

***

When Aedan showed up at The Green Witch at one o'clock the next day, Viktoria was in the backyard having her lunch. He walked past the back room window, and when he glanced out, their gazes locked.

She returned his nod of greeting. If he could be civil, so could she. They weren't enemies. They just couldn't be friends.

But as she looked in his eyes, the chemistry between them flared, and it took all her willpower to tear her gaze away from his. Thankfully, there was a lot to look at here in The Green Witch's garden. Rowan had a magick thumb when it came to growing plants and landscaping.

Designed to attract butterflies and bees as well as the appreciative eye, the garden bloomed with colour and scent. Viktoria relaxed at one of the umbrella-shaded bistro sets arranged on the terrace next to a bubbling fountain. The trickling water soothed her, and she considered it one of the many perks of working where she did.

The focal point of the garden was the ritual circle in the centre. Large enough to hold thirty celebrants, Rowan and her pagan friends, family, and clients celebrated the various pagan holidays, or sabbats, there through the year, rain or shine. The rituals were invitation only, and everyone enjoyed the potluck afterward as much as the main event.

Scattered throughout the garden, statues of goddesses and gods stood sentinel over all those who wandered through. Ever since she'd started working here and became friends with Rowan, Viktoria had considered this her second home and Rowan like a sister.

Viktoria finished the last of the salad she'd brought for lunch and checked the time on her cell phone. Still twenty minutes before she had to return to the shop and another hour and twenty minutes before her next client showed up for a reading. Reluctant to go back inside on such a glorious day, she leaned back in her chair, closed her eyes, and basked like a lizard in the sun.

The warmth of the sun's rays made her drowsy, and she dozed, flitting in and out of dreams and wakefulness. Images flashed by, slowed, and she found herself in a crowded market.

"Don't try to hide." A man's voice whispered in Viktoria's ear.

"What?" Puzzled, she turned to face the speaker.

He wore a dark robe, the hood obscuring his face with shadow. "Step out into the light where we can see you." He gripped her wrist and twisted.

"No, stop." She tried to pull away, but his grip was iron.

"You're next." He growled it into her ear. "You're mine." He pressed her close, and she struggled, not only to escape him but also to breathe.

The air thickened and she gulped, open-mouthed.

Viktoria surfaced from the dream, sweat slicking the skin on her back and chest, under her arms, drenching the blouse she wore, and greasing her hair. She knuckled the tears from her eyes, smearing mascara on her shaking fingers.

"You okay?" The voice was Rowan's.

Her gaze on the table, Viktoria nodded and gasped out, "Yes. A dream. Just a dream."

"Doesn't feel like just a dream to me." Rowan took a seat at the table beside Viktoria. "I felt the struggle all the way inside. It creeped me out."

Viktoria scrubbed her face with her hands, erasing the final dregs of the dream. "It was a dream." She said it to convince herself as much as Rowan. She grabbed her water bottle and drank half of it down. "It's hot out here."

"Don't change the subject. If he got to you here, it's my problem, too. This whole property should be a haven where no toxic energy can reach. Now he's really pissed me off." Rowan stood. "Mac won't be in for another hour, so I've got to get back. But we're not done talking about this."

"Okay." After Rowan left, Viktoria cleaned up the remnants of her lunch, washed her face in the restroom, and put the kettle on in the kitchen. Rowan was right: the two of them shared the Niko problem. No one else would believe any of what was happening, especially the accusation that respected businessman Nikolas Farkas was a—whatever he was.

As she fixed the tea, it occurred to her the only way they'd be able to protect themselves was to first figure out what Niko was.

Tea made, Viktoria picked up the two mugs and headed for the shop, anticipating discussing this with Rowan. Together they could find a way to not only protect themselves from him but rescue Eszter as well.

Hope made her heart lighter, and she picked up her pace. When she stepped from the kitchen into the back room, she almost collided with Aedan McCarthy.

CHAPTER 12

"Miss Kovacs." Aedan jumped back in time to avoid the splash of tea that slopped over the sides of each mug Viktoria held.

"Oh! I'm sorry." Viktoria froze and steadied her grip on the mugs. "Did I get you? I guess I wasn't watching where I was going."

"I guess not. No worries. You missed me." He smiled as he said it, and it reached his eyes. He swept his arm toward the door. "After you."

"Thank you." She stepped past him and through the bead curtain. "Tea, Rowan." She set the mugs on the counter.

Viktoria nipped into the back room again and wiped up the spill with a paper towel from the kitchen. By the time she returned, Aedan stood in front of the cash register with his wallet out.

"How was the reading?" Rowan rang up his total and accepted the credit card he handed over.

"Great. Seems I'm about to meet the love of my life." He raised his brows suggestively.

"Sounds as if you doubt it."

"I'm open to it." He turned to Viktoria. "I'm not interested in a serious relationship right now." He shrugged. "But who am I to argue with fate?"

Anxious for Aedan to leave, Viktoria folded her arms and tapped her foot as she stood behind the counter. To her chagrin, he didn't move toward the exit after pocketing his receipt but set a digital recorder on the counter and turned it on. He winked at her and wandered over to the book section.

Behind them, the beads rattled and Angela Demarco stepped into the shop from the back room. Her carry-on luggage-size purse hung from one shoulder, and she rattled jewelry when she walked. She'd tamed her light brown hair, always frizzy in the heat and humidity, with gel and a colourful scarf. "How was lunch, Viki?"

"Fine." She'd keep the dream she'd had between her and Rowan—at least until Aedan wasn't around.

Angela flashed a smile and headed for the door. "I don't have another client until three. Anyone need anything while I'm out?"

No one did, so Angela said goodbye and left.

Viktoria's gaze followed Aedan as he meandered around the store. Frustrated that she couldn't keep her eyes off him, she told Rowan she'd be in the back pricing stock. As she left the room, she overheard Aedan thanking Rowan for letting him hang out for the day.

So he'd be here until the store closed. Viktoria's jaw clenched. How the hell was she supposed to get any scheming about Niko done with a journalist in constant earshot? While the idea of plotting with Rowan amused her, the reality of it was deadly serious. If Niko dabbled in dark magick, as Rowan had suggested, then he'd be dangerous whether he was competent with it or not.

If he knew what he was doing, then he was possibly more powerful than Rowan, and that scared her. If he was inept, he could unleash Goddess knew what on them without the necessary controls in place.

She opened the closet where they stored unopened shipments and contemplated the stack of boxes. One of them held a gorgeous assortment of dragon and fairy figurines, and Viktoria wanted to lose herself in examining them as she sorted and priced them.

"May I help you lift that down?"

Viktoria jumped. The beads hadn't rattled, the usual signal for someone entering the back room. A further intrusion. She scowled and shook her head. "I'll manage, thanks."

"Oh, come on. Let me help you." He pointed to a box. "This one?"

She smiled. "No. If you must, grab this one." She pointed to one at the bottom of a stack.

He gave her the hairy eyeball but didn't complain and moved the boxes around until he could retrieve the one she was after.

"Thank you, Mr. McCarthy." A hint of frost edged her words. "Shouldn't you be out in the shop researching?"

"This is part of my research. I want to learn how the store functions. What you all do."

Viktoria scanned the room, spotted the pocket knife she was after on the table by the window, and strode over to get it. "Isn't your story about a psychic?"

"Yes, but she works in a store like this. Doing readings."

"Ah." Standing before him, she eyed him up and down. "Kind of a girly topic for a novel, isn't it?"

"It won't be a romance—not that there's anything wrong with that." He pulled up a chair and sat as she sliced through the packing tape on the carton.

"What made you decide to write a—what genre is it?"

"New age science fiction."

"Never heard of it." She rooted around in the beans and plastic-wrapped figures until she found the packing slip.

"It's science fiction with paranormal elements. The story will have ghosts."

"Interesting." She said it absently as she reviewed the packing slip.

"I didn't connect you to Eszter Kovacs before—the missing girl from five years ago," he said, his voice casual. "She's your sister, who you said is dating Farkas."

Viktoria went rigid and spun around to glare at him. "Correct. But I won't discuss them."

"My editor gave me the green light to do a story on Eszter's return. May I interview you about it—get the family's take on what happened?"

"Damn it. You're hanging out here to get a story—a news story. This is exactly what I suspected you of doing when you first came to me for a reading."

He faced her fury. "But I wasn't after a news story when I first came in here."

"Maybe not, but you're after one now." She dropped the packing slip, and it drifted back into the box. "Get out."

"Not this again. Viktoria, listen to me. Okay? Just listen."

She noted the use of her first name and opened her mouth to put him in his place.

A chill raced up her spine, and fear overwhelmed her. She staggered backward and would have tripped over the open box if Aedan hadn't grabbed her by the arm.

She swiped at his hands, and he released her. Reluctant to meet his gaze, she turned away. "What did Angela tell you in your reading? Did she mention Niko?"

"Nothing—no, she didn't mention Farkas."

Viktoria forced her breathing to slow and angled her head at him. "She must've said something. Angela's a good reader. I'm not being nosey. I know what I saw when I started to read for you before. What did she say?"

This time it was Aedan who turned away. He walked to the window and peered outside. "She didn't mention his name."

"But she talked about him indirectly." It was a statement. Viktoria already knew. "She told you what I told you."

"You didn't tell me much."

"I told you to stay out of his business." Viktoria wanted to scream. Her refusal to get personally involved with Aedan to prevent his possible entanglement with Niko had failed. He was scaring up the involvement, and hence the trouble, all on his own. "Why are you ignoring my warning? If you dig into his private life, if you harass him for an interview and pester my sister for one, you're doing exactly what I told you to avoid."

"I'm a journalist. That's my job description." He turned from the window and glared at her, arms crossed. "I refuse to alter how I do my job based on some nebulous hunch. Sorry." His face softened. "I've been doing this for years. Before I did the crime reporting and investigating, I went to war zones. Trust me, one asshole can't hurt me."

She shook her head. "You're a skeptic, but your mind's not as open as you claimed. Yeah, when you book the reading, you get the disclaimer this is for entertainment. But the warning I gave you was deadly serious." Viktoria moved to his side and put a hand on his arm. "Don't do this."

"If I don't, someone else will. Will you give me the interview, or do I work around you?"

Her intuition nudged her, and she tightened the grip on his arm. "Oh, my God. Are you recording this?"

"I have to record when I'm researching. Yes, I had it on when I came back here to talk to you."

"But you didn't tell me."

"You saw the recorder I set on the counter out there. It was all out in the open. Rowan's okay with it. You had no objection."

"It was out in the open then, and I was aware of it. But you're recording me now, and you hid it."

"It goes where I go. Surely you understand."

"You're planning to use what I've said against me. How do you think that makes me feel? Does it even matter to you?"

"I'll only write the truth. This isn't a vendetta against you. I don't even know you."

Viktoria released his arm. "That's the problem. What do you care if you hurt me? I'm nothing to you." She sighed. "But guess what? I care even though I don't know you either. If you do this, if you tangle with Niko, he'll hurt you."

"What can he do? At worst, he'll get a restraining order. It won't come to that. I'm not working for a gossip rag. All I want are the facts."

"And how do you get those facts? You interview him, his friends and family."

"I have the freedom to write about anyone I want, whether or not the person authorizes it. No one can stop me."

"You won't get any help from me, McCarthy. Get away from me." An uncharitable urge to shove him, hard, swept over her. Some lightworker she was. At the first sign of frustration, she wanted to jump to violence. She imagined smacking the smug right off his stupid, pretty-boy face.

Calm down. What's at the root of it?

51

She wasn't quite sure where that directive came from—perhaps her guides, or perhaps her own common-sense self—but it was a good suggestion.

Fear. She was afraid for him, and the fear was making her lash out.

Didn't it always boil down to fear? She feared losing control over her life, and he contributed to it because he refused to heed her warnings.

"You should leave, Aedan." Her voice was even, calm. She'd have to accept he'd do what he wanted, but she didn't have to help him. "I won't talk to you."

She turned back to the box and started unpacking it.

Silence blanketed the room, and, after a moment, the beads rattled as he walked out.

CHAPTER 13

"Tore a strip off you, did she?"

Aedan nodded. "She had every reason to. But I'm just doing my job."

"A handy excuse for invading someone's privacy."

He opened his mouth to retort, but she cut him off.

"I won't talk to you about my staff or their families, so don't ask. Want to know about the store or the work we do? Fine. But I won't sell out Viktoria."

"I just want to ask about your relationship with Viktoria and about her sister's disappearance and return."

"No chance. Let me give you some advice—on the house. Don't try to fool a psychic, and don't piss off a witch."

The four customers milling around the store all looked up at the same time and stared at Aedan.

He ignored the stares, held up his digital recorder, and set it on the counter. "Okay. Let me ask you this, then: you consider yourself a witch?" In his periphery, the customers returned to their browsing, but the sidelong glances they flicked his way told him they continued to eavesdrop.

"I am a witch."

"Are you The Green Witch?"

She smiled. "I'm a green witch. But if you mean the store, I'm sole proprietor, so yes, you could say I'm The Green Witch."

"Okay. What's a green witch?" He leaned on the counter.

"I work with nature, herbs, and energy flow. Since we get together for the sabbats here as a group, I'm not completely solitary, but when I work my spells, I am. Green magick respects and works with nature." She paused. "That's magick with a 'K,' by the way."

"What's the difference?"

"It's the occult spelling to separate what I do from what a magician does. My magick isn't sleight-of-hand or parlour tricks. The term used in this way originates with Aleister Crowley." She paused. "He was a British occultist. Interesting fella. Do some digging on him."

A customer approached the counter then, and Aedan stepped away to allow Rowan to conduct business. He eyed the bead curtain and almost stepped through it. Viktoria had no right to condemn him. He'd do an objective piece on the family. Hell, the work he did might even help them.

She'd insisted Niko was dangerous, yet Eszter was not just dating him as Viktoria had said. Eszter was living with him. Surely, Viktoria would want to know more about the man, and Aedan had the resources to get that information.

He took one step toward the back room and stopped. No. He wouldn't beg. There had to be a way to get her to talk to him. Going in there now would just make her angrier.

Rowan had finished with her customers, but more had entered the store. Aedan sauntered over to the books and picked one off the shelf that dealt with green witches. He'd tackle Niko's secrets another time. Perhaps he'd begin by contacting Eszter. After all, she was the one who'd gone through whatever it was that had happened.

Relief flooded through him, and a knot in his gut he hadn't been aware of released. He'd talk to Eszter, secure her cooperation, and Viktoria would realize she'd worried needlessly. Then he'd not only get the interview he wanted, he'd maybe get the sexy psychic to go out with him.

The next time Rowan was free, Aedan strode over to the counter and shot her a flirty grin. "So, gorgeous. Tell me how you became a witch."

***

Viktoria sat at a table on the patio of The Olde Tavern pub on Main Street and monitored the gate, waiting for Eszter to appear. She was tired after the emotionally draining day she'd had at The Green Witch, but the glass of red wine in front of her went a long way toward fixing that.

By the time her shift had ended, the icy wall between her and Aedan had strengthened. She'd listened to him charming Rowan, who hadn't fallen under his spell enough to violate Viktoria's trust.

Grateful to her friend for handling him, Viktoria nevertheless felt as if she'd been pressed through an emotional sieve. And now she'd have to try to convince Eszter she was living with a—Viktoria still couldn't label Niko. But she'd nevertheless have to convince Eszter he was no good for her.

Viktoria spotted her twin approaching the gate.

Eszter looked radiant. The warm, humid air hadn't wilted her as it had Viktoria. The dress Eszter wore hugged her curves, and the low neckline accentuated her breasts. A white purse that matched her strappy sandals was slung over her shoulder, and she smiled and nodded greetings to one and all as she strutted past.

When she caught sight of Viktoria, Eszter's face lit up, and she gave a spirited wave. Viktoria waved back, somewhat less enthusiastically.

Eszter slid into the chair across the table from Viktoria. "I hope the server returns soon to take my drink order. I've had a long day."

A long day doing what? Odd, she'd never asked her sister what she did for a living. "What were you up to today?"

Eszter sighed and leaned back in her chair. "Shopping. I enjoy it even though it's exhausting, so I go at least a few times a week."

"Grocery shopping?"

Eszter gave a hearty laugh. "Of course not. We have a housekeeper for that. I went downtown—Toronto," she added as though Viktoria might not realize there was only one possible downtown shopping place.

"Buy anything special?" She wasn't interested, but the small talk would fill the time.

"I found the most darling outfits and a white purse with matching shoes."

A server arrived and took Eszter's drink order for a vodka tonic. Eszter's gaze followed the server as he left, and when he was out of sight, she turned her attention back to Viktoria.

"Cute butt." She winked.

Ignoring the comment, Viktoria indicated the white bag Eszter had set in her lap and said, "Is this your new purse? It's nice."

"Oh, Lord, no. I took all my purchases home. I still have to remove the tags and go through them all."

"Why would you buy another white purse when you have a perfectly good one already?"

"Don't lecture me on it. That would be boring."

"I'm not. I'm curious. I didn't realize you were so crazy about shopping. You never used to be."

The server returned with Eszter's drink. Eszter sipped it, her face reflecting bliss. "Oh, that's good."

"I hate to nag, but should you be drinking?"

Eszter shrugged. "I'm dying. I'll do what I want."

"Aren't you fighting it?"

"The prognosis the doctors gave me sucked. If I fight it, I'll die in a year but suffer horribly from the treatment. Or I could let it ride and do what I want for the short time I have left. I choose the latter. I plan to live it up." She pulled out a pack of cigarettes. "I've taken up smoking. What's it going to do, give me cancer?"

Eszter took out a cigarette and lit up.

"I'd rather you didn't smoke. It bothers me." Viktoria waved her hands into the drifting cloud of fumes Eszter had exhaled. The smell of it already nauseated Viktoria.

"Relax. We're outside. The wind will carry it away."

"I'm downwind of you. Put it out, Eszter."

Eszter wrinkled her nose. "Fine." She rose, snatched an ashtray from a nearby table, and ground out her cigarette. "Honestly, Vik, when did you become such a baby?"

Viktoria gritted her teeth. She and Eszter hadn't always gotten along, but this self-absorbed materialist was not the sister Viktoria remembered. Was this Niko's influence?

She picked up her menu and scanned it. "I'll have the arugula salad and a burger. What about you?"

Eszter perused the menu. "Something rich. Oh, this fettuccine Alfredo looks good, with the salad. And dessert after."

A lump grew in Viktoria's throat. Maybe it wasn't self-absorption and materialism so much as fatalism.

"Eszter." Viktoria placed a hand gently over Eszter's. "What are you doing to cope with the emotional impact of your illness? Are you seeing a therapist?"

"No. My doctor recommended someone. Didn't work out. I went to one appointment and concluded it wasn't necessary." She leaned forward. "I'm not depressed. It's an inconvenience, that's all."

"Dying is an inconvenience?" Eszter's face was serious, but Viktoria couldn't believe what she'd heard. "Eszter, are you in denial?"

"Pffft. The stupid therapist tried to foist the stages of dying on me. Look, you don't understand, and I can't explain." Eszter gulped her vodka tonic, swallowing half of what was in the glass. "You need to get tested, though, Vik, to find out if you have the gene for it."

"I already did. Last year. The doctor recommended it based on our family history. It came back negative."

Eszter's eyes lit up. "Oh, how wonderful. I'm so happy for you.'

"Thank you." Viktoria frowned. Instead of filling her with love and affection, Eszter's response flooded Viktoria with an irrational fear.

To her relief, the server approached, and she flipped open her menu. After they'd placed their orders, Viktoria fiddled with her napkin as she broached the subject of Niko. "How are you and Niko?"

"Great. He's supportive, understanding—everything I could want in a man." She lowered her voice to a whisper. "We have an amazing sex life. God, I love a dominant man."

"Great." Viktoria didn't know how else to respond. How would she be able to convince Eszter her perfect man dabbled in dark magick? After a moment, an idea struck her. "Would you like to come back to my place after dinner?"

Eszter shrugged. "Sure. We'll take your car. My driver dropped me here. He can pick me up at your place later."

"I walked."

"What? Why?" Eszter looked incredulous.

"My apartment is close enough. It's a gorgeous evening."

"I'm not walking anywhere in these shoes. We'll take my limo."

Viktoria shrugged in response, uneasiness knotting her belly. She returned the subject to Niko. "What's Niko's family like?"

Eszter's expression became wary. "They're good people. All in Europe. He moved to Canada to take advantage of the real estate market here. They stayed in Romania."

"The accent is Romanian?" Viktoria bit her lip. "I thought it was Mexican."

Eszter laughed. "No, darling. He comes from a long line of Hungarian Romanians whose ancestors lived in the part of Romania that used to be part of Hungary."

"What part is that?"

"*Erdély.*"

Viktoria smothered a gasp. "Interesting."

Niko's family was from Transylvania. Maybe he was a vampire after all. She shuddered even as she dismissed the idea as ridiculous.

The server appeared with their food, and Viktoria waited while he set down the plates and verified they had everything they needed.

After he was gone, Viktoria continued to probe. "Why didn't any of his family join him here?"

"Oh, don't let's talk about Niko. I'm not in the mood. Let me tell you about the fabulous outfits I bought today." Eszter launched into a detailed description of a variety of dresses, skirts, blouses, and pants.

As her sister chattered on, Viktoria let her gaze wander outside the patio, taking in Riverwalk commons and the Holland River, which flowed into Fairy Lake. Right in front of HollisWealth Story Pod, the outdoor book exchange, she spotted Aedan McCarthy. He was staring in their direction, and he had a camera in his hands.

CHAPTER 14

The second Viktoria's gaze locked onto his, Aedan strode over to speak to her. He knew exactly what she was thinking—that he'd been spying on her. He hadn't. Well, technically you could say he was, but it wasn't deliberate.

He'd been wandering around the commons, minding his own business, when he'd turned around, and there she was, sitting on the patio at the pub and holding a glass of red wine to those luscious lips of hers. She'd mesmerized him, and he couldn't take his gaze off her.

Then she angled her chin just right and spotted him. She lifted her shades, and he caught the flare of anger in her eyes. He had no option but to confront her. No way would he allow her to accuse him of stalking her.

"Viktoria, hi." He played it as though this was nothing more than a coincidental meeting—which it was, damn it. "Long time no see," he joked.

"What a surprise." Sarcasm dripped from her voice.

"Not really. I come here often. I walk the trails, take pictures." He held up the camera as if she hadn't seen it.

"Is that so?"

"Yes, that's so." He let the irritation slip into his voice, calmed himself, and turned to face Eszter. "You must be Viktoria's sister. I've heard a lot about you."

Eszter's brows arched. "Have you?"

He held out his hand. "I'm Aedan McCarthy."

Viktoria burst into the conversation. "He's a journalist, Eszter, and he wants to do a story on you and Niko. I've tried to warn him away, but he obviously doesn't listen."

Aedan imagined her eyes flashing behind the shades she once more wore. "I'd love to do an interview with you, Eszter. Readers are interested in your story. Many times, when a woman disappears like this, it ends in tragedy. I want to give our readers your happy ending."

"Perhaps."

Viktoria's mouth dropped open. "He writes for a newspaper, Eszter. Do you want people gawking at you? Harassing you? It was awful after you disappeared. Reporters shoving mics in our faces every time we left the house." She paused. "We put up with it because we hoped the publicity would help us find you. But you're home now, and I want to be left alone."

Eszter smoothed a hand across her hair. "I don't mind a little publicity. I certainly don't mind talking to a handsome reporter." She smiled up at Aedan and sipped on her drink.

Unable to help himself, Aedan shot Viktoria a triumphant look. Some people didn't mind helping him out and trusted him to report the truth. The smirk vanished and guilt stabbed him when her face fell in disappointment.

"I appreciate you taking the time, Eszter." Ignoring Viktoria's glares, Aedan scheduled a meeting with Eszter for the following day at her home.

Trying to be magnanimous, Aedan apologized for interrupting their dinner and strolled away. He turned back once.

Viktoria's gaze tracked him. But as soon as he stepped toward her, she turned back to Eszter.

He spun on his heel and walked away.

***

It wasn't until Viktoria and Eszter settled in with a glass of wine at Viktoria's apartment that she brought up the subject of Eszter's interview with Aedan.

"Why would you talk to him?"

"He's not the first reporter who's approached me, but he's the cutest."

"That's it? He's cute?"

She shrugged. "What's it to me? People want to read about me, let them. If I don't talk to someone, they'll make stuff up."

"How will Niko react?"

"He won't mind. It's my life."

Viktoria snatched up the throw pillow next to her and hugged it. "It's Niko's life, too. They'll investigate him as well—how you met."

"Since I don't remember much, it'll be a short conversation. He's a hero, as far as the public is concerned."

"What about as far as you're concerned?"

"Of course, he's my hero, too." She frowned. "What's the matter?"

Unsure of how much to say and how to say it, Viktoria remained silent.

Eszter waited, sipping her wine and watching Viktoria all the while.

Finally, Viktoria spoke. "I don't trust Niko. He gives off a bad vibe." Before Eszter could protest, Viktoria held up her hand. "This isn't based on nothing, Ess. How well do you know him?"

"Well. We've been together for five years."

"Are you aware he dabbles in dark magick?"

Shock crossed Eszter's face. "How would you know?"

"I'm psychic. I picked up on it." She refused to get into her weird dream or to drag Rowan into the discussion.

"I'm well aware he dabbles in magick. He avoids the dark. He's a good man, Viki." Eszter stood and walked to the window. She parted the drapes Viktoria had closed when the sun had gone down and peered outside. "You don't understand what it was like for me. I was hurting, and he took me in and cared for me."

She turned her back on the window and met Viktoria's gaze. "He never hurt me, and he didn't seduce me. Sleeping with him was my decision."

Sure, with the help of a love spell or binding spell, no doubt. But Viktoria kept that to herself. "If you were having problems, would you tell me?"

"Of course. I wouldn't stay loyal to an abusive man no matter what he'd rescued me from. I'm not a victim."

"Okay." Viktoria sighed with relief, but it was short-lived. Despite what Eszter said, the nagging feeling Niko Farkas was manipulating them remained. She'd have to investigate him without her sister's knowledge. But perhaps she could draw information from Eszter. "Why don't you tell me what you do remember about what happened? Start with where he found you."

"Why are you beating that dead horse? Drop it, Viktoria."

"You were missing for five years. I need to know what happened." She dropped her gaze. "Please. Tell me what happened to you." She hated to beg as much as she hated asking Eszter to relive whatever ordeal she'd endured. But to understand Niko Farkas and expose him as the demon worshipper he was, she needed the details from Eszter.

"Very well. I'll tell you what I can." Eszter returned to the couch and sat. She picked up her glass of wine and sipped. "You have to understand, I don't remember how I got to Toronto. Everything from the time I left to the time Niko found me is a haze. I get bits and pieces, but nothing concrete."

"It's all right. Just give me what you can. I won't tell anyone—certainly not Aedan McCarthy. But I need to understand what you went through. It killed me that I couldn't find you. I tried, Eszter—I really tried." Pain twisted her gut—the same pain that had dogged her since Eszter's disappearance. She'd blamed it on worry, guilt, fear, and whatever toxic emotions had tortured her through the living hell of each day and night for the last five years.

Now that Eszter was back, she'd hoped the pain would diminish, but it had grown worse. Somehow, she had to find a way to ease the turmoil.

Perhaps discovering what had happened would help. It would certainly help her physical pain and her sister's emotional health if she could put a stop to whatever Niko was plotting.

"I wandered around downtown. The people I met dragged me into their world." Eszter hung her head. "I used drugs and hid from reality. To buy more drugs, I ..." She choked back a sob. "Why must I say it? You can intuit it, can't you? I was a mess. I didn't know where I was, who I was ..."

"I don't understand. How could you forget? Why did you run away?"

Eszter set down her wine glass hard enough to slop wine over the edge and onto the table. "I told you before, I don't fucking know! Why won't you leave it alone?" She screamed the words and leaped to her feet, making Viktoria flinch.

"Okay. I'm sorry. I'm not trying to upset you." Viktoria rose and took Eszter's hands. "What if someone—and I'm not saying it was Niko—but what if someone kidnapped you? It's awfully convenient for them you can't remember how you left home. Right?"

Eszter hesitated and gave a slight nod.

"If we trigger your memories to come back, we can report whoever it was to the police. We'll stop them. What if they're doing this to other young women?"

"It's not possible." Eszter shook her head in emphasis.

"Why? You hear about young women kidnapped into the sex trade." Viktoria's voice shook at the thought of what her sister might have endured. What if Niko was involved in that? But then why bring her home? "Do you recollect the last five years?"

"Yes."

"Why did you attempt suicide?"

"I was going through withdrawal, depression, and more pain than I could endure." Eszter sat again and picked up her wine. She heaved a sigh and continued speaking. "When your memory is gone, you have no identity. Some might believe it's a clean slate, but it's not."

"Niko said you had therapy?"

"Ha!" She said it so vehemently, Viktoria jumped. "My therapist was worse than useless. Obviously, she didn't help me at all."

Viktoria sat next to Eszter again. "So you wanted to die? What about Niko? Were you in love with him then?"

"He was wonderful. You have no idea how nice he was, how caring and attentive." Eszter's eyes shone with adoration.

Inside, Viktoria's stomach pain increased. She rose. "I have to get some water. Would you like some?"

"No, I'm good with wine."

In the kitchen, Viktoria poured herself some water from the water purifier. The apartment was quiet, the hum of the refrigerator the only sound. She took a deep breath and cleared her mind, letting it drift toward Eszter. Reading someone without their permission was an invasion of privacy, but if she didn't do it, she wouldn't be able to help her sister.

The blackness hit her immediately, almost knocking her to her knees. She gasped, clutching at the glass she held as it slid through her fingers. It didn't hit the floor, but she had a frantic moment of uncertainty where she juggled it between both hands. She set it on the counter.

Knees shaking, she gripped the counter and waited for the dizziness to pass.

CHAPTER 15

What the hell was that? The only possible answer was someone blocked her by putting psychic protection around Eszter so strong not even her twin could read her. Viktoria had struggled to tap into Eszter when she'd gone missing. The memory made her stomach churn. She'd been blocked this same way.

"Viki? What are you doing?" Eszter's voice floated out from the living room.

"Be right there." Viktoria snatched up the glass again and filled it with more water. "I guess the burger I ate made me extra thirsty. Are you sure you don't want some water?"

"What am I? A camel?" Eszter chuckled. "I'll have another glass of wine."

Viktoria returned to her seat. There had to be another way to tap into her twin. An idea struck Vikoria. "Hey, how about I give you a reading? You know—for fun?"

Eszter shook her head. "Don't be silly. Why would I want a reading?"

"Aren't you curious?"

"Not really." Eszter checked her watch. "And it's getting kind of late. I should go. Niko will be wondering why I'm out so late."

"Does he know where you are?"

"Of course, he does." Eszter set her wine glass down—the one she'd just refilled.

"You just poured that. My intention wasn't to chase you away. A reading might be fun."

"I'm not interested. I don't find it entertaining. It bores me." Eszter leaned back on the couch and crossed her ankles. "Tell me about Mom and Dad."

Surprised, Viktoria said, "Haven't you been back to visit them?"

"No. Honestly, I've been so preoccupied."

With shopping. Viktoria forced herself to release the judgemental thought, but it was difficult. How strange Eszter hadn't returned home again since that first reunion. "Have you called them?"

"No. I'll call them tomorrow." Eszter perked up. "Yes. I should go visit them. They must want to see me. It's difficult to face them, though."

"Why? They love you. It destroyed them when you disappeared. Now you're back, they want to be with you as much as possible."

When Eszter's face fell, Viktoria said, "I'm not trying to guilt you. Call them in the morning and spend a day with them. Dad retired last year. He's home all day. Drives Mom crazy, but they get along all right. They'd probably love for you to distract them."

Again, Viktoria got a sinking sensation in her gut and regretted her suggestion as soon as the words left her lips. What was wrong with Eszter visiting their parents? But the more Viktoria contemplated it, the more uneasy she became.

"You could wait until I finish work and we could go together," she suggested.

Eszter curled her legs up under her and yawned. "No, I'd rather go in the morning. Then I have your cute reporter friend coming over in the afternoon."

Oh, yes. The interview. Viktoria had her trepidations about that, too. Nothing about Eszter felt right, and it shredded Viktoria's nerves. No matter which way she turned, she was stymied. She sipped more water to clear her head.

"Don't go through with the interview, Eszter. He's bad news."

Eszter laughed. "Good one."

Viktoria smiled. She hadn't caught the pun. "I'm serious. He'll dig into our family, question you in depth about what happened to you, and ask you about Niko."

Eszter shrugged. "I don't care."

"You should."

Eszter sat up. "Why? If it doesn't bother me, why should it bother you? I can handle one reporter."

"Has there only been the one?" Viktoria found that hard to believe. Eszter's disappearance had been a big deal. Vigils had been held, searches organized. The Holland River had been dragged and so had Fairy Lake.

"Sunday we had some reporters call. A few came to the house. Niko dealt with them. He can handle anything." She held her hand out in front of her, palm down, and examined her manicure.

"So why talk to Aedan?"

"I told you."

"You said he's cute."

"Don't you think so?" She laughed. "Oh, relax. You look like you're having a heart attack. For God's sake. Do you have a thing for him?"

"If by that you mean do I want him to stay the hell away from us, then yes, I have a huge thing for him."

Eszter's laugh was as delicate as fairy song. "The sparks were flying when you two were eyeing each other. I want to learn more about him. He'll get his interview, but, in the meantime, I'll be learning about him."

"What for?" A pressure had settled on Viktoria's chest, massaging fear into her heart. An image of Aedan obscured by shadow popped into her head. Darkness closed around him until he was barely visible.

"Don't talk to him. Please. Cancel the interview."

"What's got your panties in a bunch?" Eszter grinned, and though it appeared playful, Viktoria grew cold and shivered.

"It won't go well. Don't toy with him. It's not right." Why did it seem as if Eszter was the hunter when Aedan was doing the tracking?

"You're making such a big deal over this stupid little interview. Relax. It'll be fine." Eszter set her now empty wine glass on the coffee table. "It's late. I'm tired. I'm calling my driver."

"Okay." Relieved at the prospect of solitude, Viktoria rose and picked up the wine glasses to take them to the kitchen.

From the living room, Eszter's voice rose in command as she ordered her driver to come and get her.

"Viki?" She strode into the kitchen. "He'll be here in fifteen minutes. Thanks for dinner and inviting me back here."

"Sure. We'll do it again soon."

They chatted about mundane things while they waited for the car to arrive.

After Viktoria closed the door behind Eszter, she doubled over clutching her stomach. Tears leaked from her eyes, and she dropped to her knees.

A movement across the room caught her attention. She squinted through the agony. As the room faded to black, a dark form in a hooded robe wavered and vanished into mist.

CHAPTER 16

Viktoria awoke to a throbbing headache and an aching back from lying on the ceramic tile foyer floor. The lamp she'd lit when the sun had gone down was on in the living room, but daylight haloed the curtains. She sat, rubbed the sleep from her eyes, and rose, groaning, to her feet.

How could she have spent the whole night on the floor? She hadn't drank that much. Had she? One glass of wine with dinner and another afterward, here, with Eszter. That's all.

The figure she'd seen as she'd passed out came to mind, and a chill raced up her spine, prickling the hairs on the back of her neck. She glanced at the clock in the living room: six in the morning. Her shift would begin at ten, so she had lots of time to get ready, which was good, because all she wanted to do was crawl into bed.

Spending the whole day at the store galled. She should make coffee, get some caffeine in her to chase away the exhaustion. If she got into bed now, she'd fall asleep and probably stay that way for hours, but it sure would be a relief. Oh, God, just the idea of moving exhausted her.

Viktoria stumbled to the kitchen and went through the motions of setting up the coffee maker. After that, she showered and dressed, but each step in the process took herculean effort. When at last she was ready for the day, she took her mug of coffee to the desk in her office, but logging on was too much work.

She should search the Internet for information on Niko. He was well-known enough to have an entry on the popular encyclopedia site, and she'd be able to get his bio there. But the prospect of sitting in front of the screen for what would probably turn into a couple of hours of digging daunted her.

Instead, she returned to the living room and sat on the couch to drink her coffee. The room was dim, the curtains still closed. She hadn't eaten—

no appetite. Three hours remained before she had to go to the store. Time crawled forward. She didn't have the energy or the desire to do anything and wished again she could crawl back into bed.

Aedan would likely come to the store today, and he was the last person she wanted to see. If it weren't for the four readings she had scheduled, she'd call in sick. Maybe she was sick. She certainly wasn't well. Her stomach felt as if there was a sword lodged in it.

Her cell phone rang.

Viktoria sighed. The damn thing was in her purse in her bedroom—so far away. She pictured herself getting up and walking over to get it, but that's as far as she went with the idea. The ringtone played on, and she lay down on her side and listened to it.

No need to pick up. Whoever it was could call back later. Why was someone calling at this hour, anyway? She almost sat up then, thinking maybe there was an emergency with her parents or her sister, but couldn't muster the energy.

Leave me alone. I don't want to talk to you, whoever you are.

Tears pressed close to the surface, and a lump formed in her throat. She was so alone. No one to come home to at night. No man to hold her.

Eszter was lucky to have Niko to love her, to keep her company, and to care for her. Viktoria hadn't had any serious relationships since one major crush in high school, and who'd count that? Puppy love.

Was she unlovable? Viktoria closed her eyes and let the self-pity and sadness consume her.

***

Rowan hung up the phone in her apartment above The Green Witch and called to her husband. "I'm going to Viktoria's. I'll be back in time to open the store, but I've called Mac to come in early just in case."

"No problem. Take some coffee with you. I've put it in a travel mug." Terrance Swift hurried from the kitchen and caught her before she could go down the stairs.

"Thanks, darling. I appreciate it." She accepted the mug with gratitude and headed downstairs.

Outside, all was quiet. Traffic on the street hadn't hit its peak yet. Anxiety pushed Rowan to hurry, and it was all she could do not to speed once she hit the street in her pickup truck.

Viktoria's apartment wasn't too far away—a twenty-minute drive at the most—but every stoplight slowing Rowan down increased her panic. She gripped the steering wheel tightly and hunched over it.

She'd awakened that morning with dread in her heart and terror quaking her whole body. Viktoria was in trouble, Rowan was sure of it.

The closer she got to the centre of Newmarket, the more congested it became. On Davis Drive, traffic crawled along. When a Jetta cut in front of her without signalling, Rowan swore at it. It was as close to road rage as the pacifistic Rowan ever got, and she felt guilty afterward.

Finally, she pulled into the parking lot of Viktoria's apartment building. She just hoped she wasn't too late.

***

Viktoria dragged herself off the couch at the sound of the buzzer. Whoever it was buzzing away down there would hear about it. She had a vague sense someone was in trouble but couldn't muster up the energy to care.

Why did she have to answer the door? After a while, the person wanting in would have to give up and leave her alone. Viktoria sank to the foyer floor almost in the same place where she'd spent the night. She lay her head on the cold tile and closed her eyes.

Her head still ached and her stomach burned. Oh, God, it hurt so much. Maybe she had a gluten problem. Was this how gluten-intolerant people felt? She writhed on the floor, her hands pressed against her abdomen.

The buzzing continued, a javelin spear through her temples. Why didn't that person stop? She whimpered.

Stop. Please, make it stop.

Finally, she raised herself from the floor enough to punch the button on the intercom.

"Viktoria? It's Rowan. Let me up. Please."

Unable to reply, Viktoria pressed the button to open the lobby doors and sank back to the floor. Rowan. Thank God. She could help. Viktoria should have called Rowan earlier.

The pain in Viktoria's head and gut eased up at the prospect of seeing Rowan, having her comfort and support. Viktoria curled up in the foetal position on the floor and waited for her friend to arrive.

An eternity seemed to pass before the knock on the door announced Rowan's arrival, but then Viktoria didn't want to get up. She groaned. Standing was too much for her.

Mustering all her strength, Viktoria got to her hands and knees and then slid her hand along the door until she reached the deadbolt. She opened the door, and Rowan pushed her way inside.

"Oh, Viki, my God. What happened to you?" Rowan grasped Viktoria under the arms and hauled her to her feet. "Come on. Let's get you on the couch."

In a daze, Viktoria let Rowan half-drag and half-carry her to the couch. When Rowan released her, Viktoria collapsed onto the cushions.

Rowan sat next to her. "What happened to you? I woke up this morning with a horrible sense you were in trouble. I tried to call, but you didn't answer. I'm sorry to intrude so early in the morning, but now I see you, I'm glad I followed my hunch and came over."

Tears slid down Viktoria's cheeks. "I don't know what's wrong with me. I'm so sad, so hopeless. And my head's been aching since I woke up." Too tired to say more, Viktoria lapsed into silence.

Rowan's palm traced along Viktoria's arm, to her back, and then stroked her hair. "It'll be okay. I want to do a clearing on you and put up protection."

"It's Niko, isn't it?" Viktoria's head was fuzzy, but she could think straight enough and intuit enough to know who was behind this attack—and it was an attack.

"Yes." Rowan rose. "You keep your supplies in your office?"

Viktoria nodded.

Rowan disappeared for a moment, and as soon as she left, panic engulfed Viktoria. It was as if Rowan had been a temporary shield, but without her immediate physical presence, the shield vanished.

"Hurry," Viktoria shouted. "Please. It's coming back. Oh, God, my stomach." That last was said on a groan of pain. She panted, her breath huffing out and her head dizzy. Why couldn't she just die? It would be preferable to this hell.

Then a cool hand covered her forehead, and Viktoria sighed with relief. "Thank you. Oh, thank you." She closed her eyes tight.

The sage crunched as Rowan crumbled it into an abalone shell. A match hissed as it was struck, and Viktoria caught the brief scent of sulphur in the air. The herb crackled as it ignited. Soon, the aroma of sage permeated the air.

Viktoria inhaled deeply. "The angels. I should have called the angels."

Archangel Michael, I call upon you now. Please come with your sword of light and remove any toxic cords and lower-vibrating energies from me.

As Rowan worked on smudging her, using the sage smoke to cleanse Viktoria's body, Viktoria called in Archangel Raphael for healing. The relief was instant. Why hadn't she thought of clearing herself, cutting cords and removing toxic energy, before? It should have been automatic when she'd first experienced the pain and fatigue.

She opened her eyes and saw clearly for the first time that morning.

"Can you stand?" Rowan rose as she spoke, holding the abalone shell with the sage in it in one hand and offering the other to Viktoria.

Viktoria clasped Rowan's hand and stood.

"Okay, let me smudge your whole body. Raise your arms."

Viktoria complied, and Rowan wafted the pungent herb's smoke onto Viktoria from top to toe.

When they were finished, Viktoria inhaled, pulling the air deep into her lungs, pressing it toward her abdomen. She held it for a moment and then exhaled. "Thank you. My headache and stomach ache are gone."

"You had a lot of cords on you. Don't you clear regularly?" Rowan referred to etheric cords—toxic energy links representing the dysfunctional part of a relationship between two people.

Viktoria smiled. "Not as often as I should, obviously." She hugged Rowan, holding her tight. "Thank you for coming. It was awful. I couldn't function."

Releasing Rowan, Viktoria asked her friend if she'd like to stay for breakfast. "I didn't eat, and I assume since you raced out of the house to come here, you didn't eat either."

Rowan nodded, thanking Viktoria for the offer, and the two women moved to the kitchen. Thrilled with her recovered energy levels, Viktoria told Rowan to sit and relax. "I'll take care of everything. It feels so liberating and energizing to be free of the pain and weight of that attack."

She set up the coffee maker for another pot of coffee and gathered the ingredients for veggie omelets. As she worked, she considered the implications of what she'd experienced.

"We both believe Niko is behind this, right?" Viktoria glanced at Rowan as she talked.

"Yes. Make sure you put up protection around yourself all the time. He's powerful. Take the necessary precautions."

Viktoria chopped peppers, onions, celery, and tomatoes. "What I don't understand is why he's so obvious about it." She told Rowan about the figure she'd seen the night before. "Even if you hadn't shown up, I'd have eventually realized I needed to clear and protect."

The coffee maker rumbled to a stop, and Rowan got up to fix their coffees. "He's not trying to be obvious. When you're at The Green Witch, you have protection around you by default, and I've increased it since our encounter with him. He can hammer at it and punch through to harm you, but that takes energy. Blocking you and attacking you simultaneously would weaken him."

She handed Viktoria a mug of coffee exactly the way she liked it. Viktoria thanked her and sipped, letting the slightly sweet brew do its work. She closed her eyes and savoured. When she opened her eyes, she met Rowan's studying gaze.

"Okay, that makes sense. Did he do this to Eszter before she disappeared?" If so, they'd had no defence against it at the time, and he'd been free to do as he pleased.

"Perhaps that's why you could never tap into her. He could have blocked you, and you were unaware of the obstacle. He would have put up shields around her as well, which is why I couldn't access much either—but he was focused on blocking you, specifically. I managed to get something, though it wasn't enough." Rowan returned to her seat at the table.

"Why bring her back? If he took her, why not keep her? What's in it for him if we know she's alive?" Viktoria beat the eggs, using more force as she contemplated Niko and what he might be up to.

"Honey, we'd better find out, because since she's returned, all you've had are problems." Rowan's face went white. "Viki."

Viktoria stopped beating the eggs and set the bowl on the counter. "What is it?" Her voice dripped with fear.

"Eszter's dying. What if he wants you to take her place when she's gone?"

CHAPTER 17

Rowan's suggestion that Niko would want to substitute Viktoria for Eszter when Eszter died shocked Viktoria. But she wasn't surprised. Deep inside, she'd wondered the same thing.

"That's insane," Viktoria said.

"Yes."

"Then it must be wrong." She shook her head. "He's dabbling in dark magick, but he's not crazy."

"Why not? We suspect him of attacking you psychically and of having a connection to Eszter's disappearance. Why is the idea he's after you so crazy?"

"We're not interchangeable."

"That's where I stumble, too." Rowan sipped her coffee and considered. "We need to find out what he's planning. I have an idea how."

"Okay. Tell me."

Rowan outlined her plan, and as Viktoria listened, her stomach pain returned.

***

Aedan arrived at Niko and Eszter's home at the agreed-upon time of 2:30 PM. He drove up the winding driveway to the house hidden amongst the forest covering most of the property. Enormous, the house brought to mind a Victorian mansion.

Stately columns supported a covered, wrap-around porch. The porch roof was a balcony for the second level with a smaller third story above it. The railings for both porches were painted white, the wood-frame house a salmon colour. The shutters on the windows were pale green, reminding Aedan of golf-course turf.

The majesty of it hit Aedan as he walked up the steps to the entrance. The front door opened at his knock, and a tall, heavy-set man in a uniform greeted Aedan and ushered him inside.

"Miss Kovacs is in the parlour. Right this way."

"Nice place," Aedan commented but got no acknowledgement the man had heard him.

The interior was immaculate, the floors' dark wood polished to a high gloss. The paintings on the walls were obviously originals, mostly landscapes. Aedan couldn't identify half the artists.

When they reached the parlour, the scent of fresh flowers greeted him, and he spotted multiple vases laden with a variety of blooms. Eszter sat on a French provincial sofa, and the matching coffee table was piled with pastries and service for coffee and tea.

Eszter stood and offered her hand as Aedan approached her.

"Thank you for agreeing to speak to me, Miss Kovacs."

"Please, call me Eszter."

"Eszter, then."

She dismissed the butler and motioned for Aedan to sit.

He sat on the armchair across from the sofa. Behind the sofa, French doors opened to a marble patio. The breeze blew the sheer curtains into the room in billowing clouds.

"You're prompt. I like that. We can get right to it. I've told everyone to stay out of the room while the door remains closed. Help yourself to whatever you desire." Eszter made a motion, indicating the coffee table but as if including herself. She winked at him and licked her lips.

The double entendre and innuendo shocked him, so he ignored it. "I'd like to record this, if that's okay." He smiled. "It'll help ensure I don't misquote you."

"All right." Her voice sounded identical to Viktoria's, but Eszter had a more reserved speech, as if it hinted at old-fashioned upper class. She suited the house perfectly. Even her attire spoke of tea at a garden party. She wore a strapless sundress, white with tiny flowers, and a necklace of pink pearls. A white, long-sleeved shrug covered her shoulders and arms. Strappy sandals showed off polished toes, and her legs were crossed at the ankles.

Aedan was surprised she wasn't wearing white gloves and a sunhat.

He dug his digital recorder out of his briefcase, turned it on, and set it on the coffee table between them. "Why don't we start with your background? Tell me about your life before your disappearance."

Eszter poured herself some tea and fiddled with honey and milk. "I had just finished my second year of university. My major was philosophy, but I had a minor in English literature. I was attending the University of Waterloo. I'd lived in residence the first year, but for the second year, I moved into a house with three friends." Her eyes became distant, and her voice grew fainter. "We had fun, but I spent a lot of time studying. After the first wild semester, I chose to take school more seriously."

She put a muffin and two cookies on a small plate and nibbled on them before continuing.

Aedan took the opportunity to fix himself a coffee. He eyed the pastries and decided against having one. "Please, continue."

She smiled, showing teeth. For a moment, he almost expected vampire fangs. He shook his head. Nonsense.

As twins, Viktoria and Eszter's faces were strikingly similar, but only if you examined them closely. Eszter's heavily made-up face masked the similarities. Did Viktoria wear makeup? If she did, it was so subtle as to be invisible. And Viktoria never made him think of vampires.

"I remember packing and getting ready to leave. My boyfriend planned to drive me home."

"Your boyfriend?" None of the news reports he'd read had mentioned a boyfriend.

She shrugged. "A guy in the philosophy program. It wasn't serious. We never slept together. When I disappeared, I was a virgin."

Aedan shivered, suddenly chilled. "Did your parents know of him?"

"No."

"Did you tell the police about him?"

"No. If you're thinking he's responsible for what happened, you're wrong. I left on my own."

"I thought you couldn't remember how you got to Toronto?"

She sipped her tea, slurping delicately. "I don't. But my boyfriend—we'll call him John—"

"Is that his name?"

She smiled. "No. I won't give you his name. He doesn't need the hassle."

Aedan shrugged. He could dig and find out. Records of Eszter's stay in residence and lists of her classmates wouldn't be hard to get. He'd talk to anyone who might have come into contact with her during that time. Someone would get chatty enough to spill it.

"The police would have questioned your friends. Did they question your boyfriend?"

"Detective Baker did. He won't give you John's contact info."

"That's all right." Aedan would see about that. "So what happened? You finished packing to go home?"

"Yes. And then I was in Toronto. I remember a bus ride, come to think of it." She squinted at him. "Funny. I've never recalled that before."

"Were you alone?"

"People were on the bus."

"Yes, but did any of your friends go with you?"

"I can't say."

"Can't? Or won't?"

"Can't. Sometimes I get bits and pieces—flashes of memory. Mostly I don't want to go back there. It was a dark time."

"In what way?"

"I was depressed. Lost. I won't think of that time—couldn't if I tried—but most of all, I don't want to peek behind that curtain." She sipped her tea, nibbled a cookie. "My first real memory of that time was struggling to escape from two men who wanted to rape me and Niko fighting them off."

"He fought them? Physically intervened?"

"Yes. He's skilled in martial arts."

Aedan raised his brows. "He's a man of many talents."

She raised her shoulders in a feminine shrug. "He's studied many disciplines. Whatever he wants to learn about, he dedicates himself to and masters. He's driven and ambitious."

"The world views him as a businessman."

"Yes." She set her cup and saucer on the coffee table and curled her legs under her. "I'm honoured he came to my rescue. He could have left me to their mercies. Or he could have stopped them but left me on the streets. He brought me here and personally nursed me back to health and sanity."

Her eyes glinted in the sunlight as she angled her head toward the patio doors. "We fell in love."

Yet she'd flirted with Aedan—perhaps that was her style—again, so different from her sister. Viktoria was so down to earth, Aedan couldn't picture her flirting with him even if she wasn't mad at him every time he saw her.

"But you didn't remember your family at all?"

"No. But the more time Niko and I spent together, the more that didn't matter. He didn't care if I knew my real name. He loves me, and I love him."

"How long were you living here before you realized it?"

"A few months." She gave him a thin-lipped smile. "He's a sexy man. Compelling. I was drawn to him immediately. He was so kind and gentle." There was longing in her voice. "He's always taken care of me."

"Yet you tried to kill yourself."

She gasped. "Where did you hear that?"

"I have my sources."

She averted her gaze, rose, and went to the window, absently stroking the inside of her left forearm. "I had some dark days in the beginning. That's when I tried to kill myself. Once again, Niko saved me."

"He sounds like a great guy."

She turned and faced him. "He is. Despite what my sister might have told you."

Aedan seized the opening. "What does Viki have against Niko?" He used Viktoria's nickname. If Eszter assumed he had a close relationship with Viktoria, perhaps she'd divulge more, forget this was for a story.

"She makes assumptions. If you're as close to her as you allude, she'd have ranted about it to you already." Eszter smirked, and he knew she'd seen through his little ploy.

He changed tactics. "You have a lovely home. Is this where you've stayed since Niko rescued you?"

"Yes. At first I had my own room. Now, of course, we share."

"You're telling me you've lived in Newmarket for five years and never crossed paths with Viktoria or your parents?"

"I live in this house, but I don't spend a lot of time in town. It's possible we passed by each other and didn't realize it."

"She searched for you."

Eszter ran her fingers through her hair, smoothing it down. "Yes, but I wasn't looking for her, and I told you, I don't spend much time in town. I shop in Toronto. Or we travel. When I was well enough, we toured Europe, visited his family."

"What are your plans for the future?"

Immediately, her expression turned to one of despair, and she buried her face in her palms. Startled to see her shoulders shaking with sobs, Aedan jumped up and went to her. He put a hand on her shoulder, trying to offer comfort and sympathy.

"I'm sorry. What did I say?"

"It's not your fault," she said, her voice tear-drenched and muffled.

"What is it?"

Eszter raised her head from her hands and stared into his eyes. "I'm dying. We have no future together. All he can do is keep me company until the end." She said it matter-of-factly with no hint of self-pity.

"I'm so sorry. What happened?"

"Breast cancer. Genetic."

The words made his stomach clench and he instantly feared for Viktoria. Eszter must have caught the direction his thoughts were taking, because she shook her head. "Just me."

"How do you know? You're twins. Wouldn't the odds be against Viktoria?"

"She was tested last year. I already asked her about it."

Relief coursed through Aedan. Viktoria was okay. "How did you recover your memories?"

She returned to the sofa and sat again, curling her legs under her. "When the doctor gave me the diagnosis, I was shocked, horrified. It was enough to trigger a memory of my name, and from that, a memory of my parents, of Viki. Niko hired a private investigator to find my family, and that's how we discovered I had been reported missing."

"Your mother's health is fine, isn't it?" Once again, he took the seat across from her.

"So far. But her mother died of it, and one of her two sisters also. Between me and Viki, I drew the short straw, I guess."

"I'm sorry."

"We're coping."

"Are you getting treatment?"

"I'm refusing treatment. My reasons. I won't get into them with you. Sorry." She poured herself more tea and doctored it.

Behind Aedan, the door opened. He started to turn and see who'd entered but knew when he caught the burst of delight on Eszter's face.

Niko Farkas had arrived.

CHAPTER 18

Niko Farkas dominated the room with his presence the moment he stepped into it. He held out a hand to Aedan, and the grasp, when Aedan rose and they shook hands, was firm, cool, and dry. Aedan invited Niko to join them, but he declined.

"No time, I'm afraid. I'll need to ask you to wrap it up."

"Would you be willing to give me a statement about Eszter? How you found her, how you helped her."

"I'm sure she's told you already. I will say I love her and will do anything to help her." He motioned to the butler, who stood waiting in the hallway. "Bernard, please escort Mr. McCarthy to his car."

"Please, it's Aedan." Aedan put away his recorder, grabbed his briefcase, and shook Eszter's hand. "Thank you for your time. I appreciate it."

"I'm sure you'll do the story justice, Aedan."

Aedan said his goodbyes and followed Bernard from the room.

***

When the front door closed, Niko strode to Eszter's side. "Talitha. My love. How did it go?"

"Fine, my heart."

"You covered all the points we discussed?"

"Yes. I had to wing it a bit, but everything went pretty much as expected."

"You flirted, my pet?"

She batted her lashes in response. "As only I can." She wrapped her arms around him, pressed against him. "When will this be over, Niko? I'm tired. I need out of this body."

"Patience, my dear. We're dealing with someone who is aware—not an unsuspecting innocent as Eszter was."

"Five years wasted." She pulled away and frowned at him.

"It was a coin toss. We won't make that mistake again. Who'd have predicted this body was so susceptible to a disease of old age?"

"Not always old age." She pursed her lips, thinking it over. "The odds were with us. The mother was fine."

"Did the reporter verify his attraction to Viktoria?"

"He pretended to be closer to her than he is, but I could see the desire for her in him. Viktoria will fall for him. She's a sucker for love." Eszter laughed but quickly sobered again.

"What is it?" Niko worried about her. The doctors had told them she had two months if she didn't receive treatment, so they'd have to hurry. After all, it took a lot of effort, planning, and time to steal someone's body, and Viktoria was already suspicious. If she discovered what they were after, they'd be forced to kill her sooner than they wanted to.

Damn psychics. Why couldn't Viktoria Kovacs be as mundane as her sister had been? Eszter had been easy to capture. She'd walked into their trap with open arms and a trusting mind. Before she'd realized what was happening, she'd lain bleeding to death on the table in his lab.

If everything went as planned, they'd have Viktoria in the same place within a week. His sweet Talitha was so tired all the time now. Eszter's body was losing its fitness and wasting away. Niko anticipated ravishing Talitha in Viktoria's hot little body. The girl had some meat on her, those breasts more than a handful.

Niko grew hard in anticipation. "I hope you're not too tired, Tally. Let's go upstairs for a while."

She met his gaze and licked her lips. "My Niko. I'm yours, as always."

***

Since they'd agreed to wait until Sunday after the store closed to implement Rowan's plan, Viktoria made sure she cleared and protected herself every morning and night. Rowan insisted on doing it again before Viktoria left the store even if it was just to run to the supermarket.

Aedan hadn't been around since the day of her dream, much to Viktoria's relief, but when she walked into work Thursday morning, there he was. She caught herself frowning at him out of habit and forced her face to relax.

"Good morning, Viktoria."

"Aedan." She scanned the shop. "Where's Rowan?"

"Making tea. She'll be out in a moment."

"She trusted you here alone? Maybe I should pat you down."

He grinned at her, and it made him look boyish. "Be my guest."

Her face flushed, and she regretted uttering the words. "It's okay. I'd sense if you'd taken something. We don't need security cameras here—only when the store is closed."

Aedan perked up. "Oh, yeah? You can tell if someone shoplifts?"

"Yes. People give off their intention, and once they've swiped whatever it is they're after, their aura changes. There's guilt associated with committing a crime or doing something sneaky. It shows up in the aura."

"What if the person is a psychopath and has no conscience? Sociopaths don't feel guilt, from what I understand. Would you still know?"

The question took her by surprise. Fascinated, she considered. "Yes, because they'd feel triumph. It would still show, but in a different way. Excellent question."

A woman entered the store, and Viktoria greeted her and asked if she needed any help. Throughout the morning, Viktoria did two readings, stocked the shelves, and served customers. It was almost lunchtime before the activity in the store calmed down enough to leave Viktoria, Rowan, and Aedan alone.

Viktoria opened her mouth to confront him about the interview he'd done with Eszter when the bell on the front door jingled, signalling a customer. She pressed her lips together, itching to talk to him but unable to in front of strangers.

As she attended to the customer's needs, a few more people entered the store. Viktoria glanced at the time. She could go for lunch soon. Working quickly, she handed change back to the person whose order she'd just processed.

CHAPTER 19

Before anyone else could approach the till, Viktoria called out to Rowan, "Mind if I go for lunch now, Ro?"

"Sure. Give me a minute, and I'll take over." Rowan rose from a place on the floor in front of a shelf where she'd been rearranging crystal singing bowls. She left the room as another customer reached the counter to check out.

Viktoria smiled at the young man and started ringing up his purchases. As they chatted about the interesting items he'd found, Viktoria sneaked a peek at Aedan.

Though Aedan had spent most of the morning following Rowan around, asking her about process, listening and watching as she waited on customers, he hadn't ignored Viktoria. He'd spent less time observing her, mostly staying out of her way, but, on occasion, he'd trained his attention on her. Each time he had, she'd been hyper-aware of it.

When his gaze followed her, she sensed it, and they'd locked eyes frequently. To her exasperation, she'd blushed more often than not, the self-conscious flush warming her face. He smiled disarmingly at her every time, and she'd had to force herself to focus on what she'd been doing before she'd caught him staring.

As long as she concentrated on the argument they'd surely have when she finally cornered him about Eszter, he didn't fluster her. But always, when she first met that penetrating gaze, her mind went blank, and she found breathing difficult. Damn him.

Rowan returned and slipped behind the counter. "Okay, away you go." She set a mug of tea next to the till and scanned the shop, getting a bead on everyone in the store.

"Thanks, Rowan. I'll be in the backyard. It's a nice day to eat outside. By the way, I'm dragging the reporter out with me. He's got some explaining to do."

Rowan winked at Viktoria. "Journalist."

Viktoria grinned in return. "Yeah. Whatever."

She strode to Aedan, who was poking around in the box of assorted crystals.

He held one up as she reached him. "Tiger's eye, according to the label. What's it mean?"

She was tempted to shrug and tell him to ask Rowan, but that would be rude. He might be a pain in the neck, but he'd asked a legitimate question. She took the stone from him and held it in her left hand.

"This stone has grounding and protecting properties." She turned it over in her palm, studying the gold, light brown, and mahogany striations. Interesting he'd picked this one. "It boosts psychic ability." She ignored an urge to place it over her third eye right then. "Some people use it as a talisman."

"What does a talisman do, exactly?"

"Bring luck or ward off evil." She put it back in the box and made a mental note to put on her tiger's eye necklace when she got home. Viktoria cast her gaze on Aedan.

He met it with that smile he'd been sending her way all morning, and her body reacted with a thrill of electricity.

"Let's go outside. I want to talk to you."

Aedan responded with a nod and an expression of curiosity.

On their way out, Viktoria grabbed the lunch she'd brought with her from the fridge in the kitchen. "Did you bring your lunch?"

When he shook his head, she experienced a stab of guilt and said, "I'll share." No sooner had she said the words than she mentally kicked herself. They'd have to eat before she argued with him. No, that logic was lunacy. Why should they argue? Did she have to construe everything he did or said as an attack or affront to her?

They sat at one of the bistro tables, and Viktoria took a few minutes to set up the meal. She rushed back into the kitchen, got them two bottles of water, plates, and utensils, and then laid out the food.

"I prefer to eat vegetarian. I hope you don't mind."

She set a bowl of kale and broccoli salad on the table, a container of sliced cheeses, and another of muffins she'd made. "I usually bring enough to share."

"Looks great. What are the muffins?"

"Just plain." She took out a small bowl of fruit salad and removed the lid. "Help yourself."

"Thank you." He picked up a plate and served himself but gave her sidelong glances as he did. "I have a feeling I'll have to sing for my supper. What did you want to discuss with me? Or should I ask so soon?"

She sighed. "I'm not interested in fighting with you."

"Good, because I'm not interested in fighting with you, either."

"Okay." She picked up the remaining plate and scooped some salad onto it, following that with cheese and a muffin. "Since you brought it up, tell me what you and Eszter discussed, what you said about me, and what you plan to publish."

"Let's get one thing clear." He set his fork down. "I don't owe you an explanation for anything I do, and I certainly don't owe you a recap of what was said in an interview."

When she opened her mouth to protest, he held up his hand. "What Eszter told me was between me and her."

Viktoria dropped her fork and leaned back in her seat. "And everyone who reads your newspaper."

"Whatever she told me that's relevant to the piece, yes, but it won't cause you problems. She told me you'd had the genetic testing done. I was relieved to hear your tests came back negative for the breast cancer gene." His gaze never left her as he picked up his fork and started eating again. "The salad's excellent. I never expected to enjoy kale. It even sounds like goat food."

She smiled. "This salad's not too heavy-handed with the kale, and the dressing gives it just the right tang." She leaned forward, picked up her fork, and took a few bites.

"I met Niko."

Viktoria froze, mid-chew, and waited for him to continue.

"He didn't say much to me. Kicked me out as soon as he got there. I got the feeling he didn't want to talk to me."

"Imagine someone not wanting to talk to a reporter."

He frowned, annoyed. "I'm not a—"

"Yeah, yeah. You know what I meant."

He picked up a napkin and wiped the corner of her mouth. "Just a little dressing right there."

The touch was intimate, and Viktoria wanted to take his hand and stroke it. Instead, she let him finish and then leaned back in her seat.

"Thank you." Her voice was a whisper, blending with the trickle of the water fountain and the tinkling of the fairy bells from the tree branches.

A light breeze wafted across the heat of the day, bringing with it the scent of roses from the trellis beside them. Across the grass, at the ritual circle's edge, a hummingbird buzzed among the honeysuckles.

Viktoria's stomach unclenched, and it wasn't until it did that she realized how much tension she'd held in her body. She didn't know much about the man sitting across from her who was prying into her life.

"Tell me about yourself, Aedan." If she focused the conversation on him, it would keep them from talking about her and her family.

"Not much to tell. I grew up in Toronto. Went to Ryerson for journalism. Got my degree. Worked the newspapers—managed to land a job at the big Toronto paper. Did a stint in New York. It was the place to be at the time." He chewed a bite of food and took a swig of his water. "When it stopped being the place to be for me, I came home."

"When was that?" She twisted the cap off her water bottle and chugged.

He grew quiet again, his expression sad. "Nine-eleven."

She gasped and thudded the bottle down next to her plate. "You were there?"

"In the neighbourhood. I saw the first plane hit, but I was too far to get there. I went after the story and raced to the scene to go into the building.'

"Are you crazy?"

"At the time, I didn't understand what had happened, and I didn't think."

"Clearly." Fear of what might have happened made her snap at him. If he'd died that day, they'd never have met. Shame at the way she'd spoken to him washed over her. "I'm sorry."

He frowned, puzzled. "For what?"

"Our paths have crossed, and I didn't understand how lucky that makes me. If you'd died then, we wouldn't be sitting here together—we'd never have met." That one decision could have changed everything, and she'd have been oblivious.

Aedan smiled. "Thank you. But by the time I got near enough, the second plane had hit, and no one could get into any of the buildings except police and firefighters. I recorded, observed, and helped where I could. We had to run for our lives when the buildings started to collapse. I took shelter in a store, pulling people in with me so they wouldn't die in the street buried in toxic dust. I feared we might die anyway. The horror of that day will never leave me."

The air stilled and the sun disappeared behind a cloud. Viktoria shivered despite the heat and humidity. A shadow obscured Aedan's features, making her gasp and recoil. His handsome face morphed into a grinning skull.

CHAPTER 20

When Viktoria jumped backward, she knocked her bottle of water off the table and into her lap. Water soaked into her skirt, and the wet chill of it made her leap to her feet.

Aedan, face normal once more, leaped from his chair and rushed to her side. "What happened? You look like you've seen a ghost."

He made a move to grasp her arm as she stumbled over her chair, but she reflexively batted his hand away.

"I'm okay." She gripped the table to keep from falling. When she'd recovered her composure, she bent down to pick up her bottle.

"Most of it's on my skirt," she said and screwed the cap back on. "Just water. It'll dry." She tried to squeeze out any excess by wringing the wet part in her hands, but nothing dripped out.

"What's wrong, Viki? You act like you're afraid of me." A mix of emotions showed on his face.

She raised her eyes to meet his gaze. "I—no, not afraid." She wasn't. What she'd seen had to do with him, and it was a warning.

"Then what? It involved me, didn't it?"

She gave him one reluctant nod.

"Then tell me what happened." He stepped closer to her, and it took all her self-control not to retreat.

"You wanted to step back." His voice was laced with concern. "Why?"

"A vision scared me."

"What?" His voice rose in angry frustration. "You may as well tell me. I won't let you worm out of it."

"Nice. Very charming."

"Don't deflect. What did you see?"

She sighed. "A skull. Superimposed on your face."

"Jesus." He brushed a hand through his hair. "What does that mean?"

Viktoria averted her gaze.

"Please. Tell me." Now his voice held fear. "Will I die?"

That broke through her defences and her heart went out to him. "No. I'm so sorry you thought that. It's more of a psychic attack. An intrusion into our conversation."

She pondered. "I'm not sure why." What had they been discussing? The events of nine-eleven. "Coincidence?"

"What do you mean?"

"When you told me you were in New York that day, I realized how close to danger you were. It reminded me how fragile life is, how lucky I am our paths crossed at all."

"What does that have to do with my face turning into a skull?"

Into a grinning skull, she mentally corrected him—but she wouldn't tell him that. He was freaked out enough. "Nothing. Probably."

"Why probably? What aren't you telling me?"

"Aedan, I warned you to stay away from Niko. You didn't listen to me. Don't write the story."

He planted his fists on his hips and frowned. "I hope you're kidding. My editor's waiting for me to deliver it to him. I've got a deadline of tomorrow morning."

"And yet you've been hanging out here?"

His expression grew cold. "Just for the morning. Thanks for lunch, but it's time I went to work on my story. Have a nice afternoon."

He turned on his heel and walked away, leaving Viktoria standing with her mouth hanging open.

***

She'd been rude to him again. Viktoria wrestled with the guilt as she cleaned up the remains of their lunch. Why did she have to get so hostile? He was just doing his job. Yes, and his job was the crux of the problem. He was messing with her private life, with her sister, her family.

Well done, Vik. If he planned to hold back any of it for your sake, you've kyboshed that now, haven't you?

She could call him and apologize, but with her luck, she'd make it worse. No matter what she said or did, they fought.

Viktoria verified the backyard was clean. She washed and put away the dishes and then returned to her chair on the patio. Before her lunch hour ended, she wanted to reflect on what had just happened and figure out what, if anything, it meant.

She suspected it meant Niko was messing with her again but couldn't prove it.

For all she knew, she was losing her mind, or she'd received a message about Aedan after all and had misread it. She forced herself to organize her thoughts. Ways to distinguish true Divine guidance from false existed. All she had to do was take the steps to figure out which this one was.

Start with feelings. How had she felt? It had startled her, and yes, it had frightened her. As a matter of fact, it had frightened her so much she'd leaped away from Aedan. When he'd tried to approach her or touch her, she'd immediately smacked his hand away. Yet she'd told him she wasn't afraid of him.

He hadn't been the cause of her fear. The skull had obscured his face, but it hadn't been his face, hadn't represented him.

She closed her eyes and relaxed. Perhaps if she meditated on it, she could figure it out. Instantly, uneasiness twisted her stomach and she opened her eyes. What if the dream she'd had before returned?

Annoyed, she went through the steps of clearing and protecting herself. Damn it, she knew how to keep toxic energy out, whether it was Niko or someone else. He had no place here. Better, she closed her eyes again and breathed in and out, focusing on her abdomen until she relaxed.

Images passed in and out of her consciousness: a locked door; Aedan, offering her a red rose; a poison symbol; Rowan, unconscious; Eszter, her head morphing into a black dog's head; a skeletal hand reaching for Viktoria …

She snapped back to full awareness. What the hell was all that? Again, nothing had been clarified. Viktoria stood and stalked into the house, fixed herself a cup of tea, and went back to the store.

A few customers wandered among the shelves. Rowan was completing a transaction with a short, stout woman Viktoria didn't recognize. When the customer left, Viktoria suggested to Rowan she take lunch, and Rowan went out.

Alone in the store except for three looky-loos—Viktoria could always tell when they wouldn't buy anything—she made a list of the images she'd seen. After reviewing the list, she made a decision. When the store closed, she would demand to implement Rowan's idea that night. Niko Farkas was not going to harass her again. Viktoria had had enough.

***

Rowan finished closing up the till and motioned for Viktoria to follow her to the kitchen. Before flicking off the lights in the store, Rowan surveyed the room one last time: closed sign facing out, front door locked, till closed and everything in order. Rowan held the bead curtain out of the way, and Viktoria stepped past her into the back room.

After shutting and locking the back room door, Rowan went to find Viktoria.

In the kitchen, Viktoria poured tea into the teapot. "I'll put out the leftovers from lunch."

"How long will this take?" Rowan checked her watch. Her husband worked afternoons and wouldn't be home until ten-thirty at least, but she'd planned a wild night of watching Star Trek reruns.

"Maybe hours." Viktoria looked sheepish. "I'm sorry, Ro. It's an imposition, but something happened this afternoon."

Rowan experienced a sinking sensation in her stomach, and her hands grew cold. "What is it?"

As the two women set food out on a table in the backyard and made tea, Viktoria told Rowan about her lunch with Aedan.

"I've made a list of the images." She reached into her skirt pocket and removed a small slip of paper.

Rowan sat in a chair and held her hand out.

"Before you read this, I should tell you one of the images I saw was you."

"Yes?" A chill went up Rowan's spine at Viktoria's worried expression. "I won't blame you for what popped into your head. Let's have it, Viki."

"You were unconscious."

"What else?" Rowan kept her voice steady. She refused to let this rattle her. It might be nothing.

"That's all."

"Okay." Rowan let out the breath she was holding and let her shoulders drop. "What was the feeling associated with it?"

Viktoria sat down across from Rowan and propped her chin on her hand. After a moment, she sat up and said, "Danger. Around you. Serious. Harm will come to you."

"Did you sense involvement from anyone else?"

"It always goes back to Niko. We need to deal with him. I can't hold him off indefinitely."

"Let me see that list."

When Viktoria handed it to her, Rowan scanned the items. "The red rose from McCarthy isn't bad news."

"I guess it depends on how you interpret it, doesn't it? Red roses represent romantic love, and I don't want to get involved with him."

"You're attracted to him, and he's attracted to you. Do you deny it?"

"No. But every time we're together, we end up arguing. I insult him, or he makes me angry. Usually he makes me mad first, and then I get rude."

"Sexual tension." Rowan had seen it the moment the two first locked gazes.

Viktoria scoffed.

Rowan let it go. Viktoria could deny it all she wanted, but she would get romantically involved with Aedan McCarthy. It was destined to be.

Rowan was certain this was one of those glimpses of the future that could not be changed. The will was free, and they could dance around a relationship all their lives if they wanted to. But in this life or the next, they'd be together. Sometimes, destiny took its sweet time.

"You want me to do the scrying tonight, don't you?" Rowan wasn't crazy about implementing her idea on such short notice, but if that's what was needed, she'd do it.

Viktoria met Rowan's gaze straight on. "Yes. It's a lot to ask, and you haven't had any time to prepare. But he's busting through my defences. Whenever I try to meditate, he intrudes. I haven't been able to access my guides because of him."

Rowan nodded. "I've been adding to your protection, and if he's still getting through, you're right—we must act. I'll need your help."

"Of course."

"We'll set space in the circle. We'll call the quarters and the lord and lady. We must ensure he can't see us or touch us while we do this." A twinge of nerves made Rowan want to put it off for another day. What if Niko's powers were stronger?

Viktoria's vision had been a warning, Rowan was sure of it—another glimpse into the future, this time, Rowan's destiny. The reading she'd done for herself, the one she'd refused to share with Viktoria, had given her the same danger warning.

She hadn't lied, exactly, when she'd said Viktoria wasn't involved. After all, it wasn't Viktoria causing the danger. She was caught in it but not responsible for it. Rowan had hoped it would pass them by, though she'd understood even then darkness encroached.

Now, they needed to learn what Niko was doing or he'd win. At least she could do her part to prevent that, no matter what it ended up costing her.

He had no right to take what wasn't his, and Rowan was certain he was here to take Viktoria.

CHAPTER 21

They finished their meal and then cleaned up and put away the dishes.

As the sun went down, Viktoria and Rowan set up the ritual circle with an altar table and a chair for Rowan. A black cloth covered the altar and Rowan placed her crystal ball on its stand in the south quadrant of the table.

Both wearing ritual gowns and hooded capes and both barefoot, they set the space.

Rowan cast the circle using her sword and walking deosil, or clockwise, around the edge, starting in the northeast. When Rowan returned to stand before the altar, Viktoria picked up the witch's broom, or besom, and swept the circle, also clockwise and also starting in the northeast. Next, they did the purifications, once around the circle with the incense, Rowan beginning in the east, for air. A candle represented fire, and Rowan carried it around the circle from the south gate.

Viktoria took water and earth, starting at the west gate with a water-filled seashell and then carrying a rock with salt on it around the circle from the north gate. The quarter calls were done, again in order of east, south, west, and north. So the spirits of air, fire, water, and earth were called into the circle.

A light breeze, a wash of heat, a hint of humidity, and an awareness of the solid ground under her feet alerted Viktoria to their presence.

Rowan blessed and consecrated the circle, making it a shield against evil and a defensive wall to preserve and protect them.

Once that was done, the two women met in the centre, at the altar, and invoked the god and goddess. The energy in the circle increased as the lord and lady entered the sacred circle. The two mortal women blessed the wine and offered a libation to the gods.

Rowan sipped from the chalice and then offered it to Viktoria.

The sweet mead flowed into her mouth, and she savoured the taste. She smiled, and her heart filled with love and affection for Rowan.

"We'll begin," Rowan said and took her seat at the altar in front of the crystal ball. "Stand behind my chair and protect me."

The sun had set; all was wrapped in velvety darkness.

Viktoria took her position behind Rowan and focused on enhancing the protections already in place.

Before her, Rowan sat, back straight, gazing into the crystal. To Viktoria, the crystal ball was clear and reflected the stars, the sliver of a moon, and the flicker of the candle sitting on the altar. But to Rowan, it had probably already gone misty. When the mist cleared, the images would come.

Powerful enough to control the direction the images would take, Rowan would home in on Niko and Eszter. Through scenes that played out like a movie, Rowan would learn who Niko was, what he was doing, and why.

Of course, he'd have his own protections up, and so it would become a battle of wills. The risk was he'd sense their intrusion and retaliate.

Rowan's expression changed. In a low, meditative voice, she began to speak. A digital recorder, their one concession to modern technology, captured every sound. In her trance, Rowan wouldn't comprehend most of what she said, so it would help them both to listen to the replay later.

"He's old. Originating in Transylvania."

Viktoria waited. Eszter had told them that much.

"Before it was part of Hungary."

Viktoria gasped. Impossible. He'd have to be—how old? *Vampire.* No. She wouldn't consider it. Ridiculous. But the doubts persisted. She'd seen him out and about in the daytime.

Maybe he sparkles, she thought, mockingly.

"The Romans conquered it, and after the Romans, the Magyars. Niko was born during the Roman conflicts."

Rowan continued, her voice flat. "Sorcerer. He comes from a long line of them. They work in secret, against the empire. They are persecuted but have power to cloak and shield themselves. His face is different, but I recognize his energy."

As Rowan spoke, the words painted pictures in Viktoria's mind, and she saw tortures, burnings. The people who suffered were those who lived in the countryside. The peasants. The pagans.

But Niko's family endured—the ones who'd survived the clashes with the Roman soldiers. Certainly, Niko had. He grew from boyhood to manhood, and it was then his grandfather taught him the old family secrets of sorcery.

Niko learned with an enthusiasm born from a thirst for knowledge and a hunger for power. Before long, he'd out-paced his father and his grandfather. The student became a master. But where his sires had wanted to exist in secret and survive, Niko had wanted to rule, to control. He turned from the light to dabble completely in the dark, and when his grandfather tried to stop him, Niko killed him.

In the visions flashing through Viktoria's horrified mind, she watched Niko amass wealth and power. He'd fallen in love with the daughter of a landowner. Talitha. As cruel and ambitious as Niko, she married him, and when her father died, murdered her older brother so she'd inherit everything. When Niko reached old age, he determined to find a way to keep what he'd worked so hard to acquire by extending his life.

Rowan gasped. "Talitha. She's—"

A loud roar of wind drowned out Rowan's voice. The images splintered and vanished.

Viktoria scanned the circle. A force pressed against the cone of energy they'd raised. She walked the perimeter, pushing energy outward to strengthen what they'd built.

Rowan hunched over the crystal ball. Her face white, Rowan's lips moved as she continued to dictate what she saw.

In her periphery, Viktoria glimpsed movement and turned her attention to the area beyond the borders of their circle. Shadows slinked in the darkness beyond, figures darker than the night's ink. Inside the protection of the circle, the air was warm and comforting. Outside, an icy mist rose from the grass, dusting plants, trees, and rocks with frost.

Whatever was out there was fighting to break down the energy barrier and enter the circle.

Viktoria grabbed the sword from beside the altar and walked the circumference clockwise, sending energy to reinforce the circle. She called on the elementals to assist her, and the god and goddess to protect and guide her. "The sun brings light, and the moon holds darkness. As above, so below. Lord and Lady, help your children."

A multitude of shadow creatures pressed against the circle, but Viktoria held them back. She glanced at Rowan again. If Rowan didn't stop scrying soon and help out, Viktoria feared the circle would collapse in on her.

Outside, the shadows flowed widdershins, or counter-clockwise, trying to drag her circle down. Shrieks and cackles serenaded their attempts.

Fear hammered Viktoria's heart. She forced herself to breathe and trust the energy they'd raised was enough and the help they'd asked for had been granted. The hot, humid air had sweat streaming down Viktoria's back and under her breasts. The exertion took a toll, and her pace slowed.

When she realized she'd almost stopped, she forced her feet forward. She gripped the sword in both hands and continued to chant. "Lord and Lady, help your children."

A light flashed across the circle, the beam cutting through the darkness onto the shadow creatures.

Horrified, Viktoria recognized Aedan's car. "Oh, no. Oh, Goddess, make him leave. What is he doing here?"

What would she do? She couldn't leave him to the mercy of the shadows, but if she cut a door and went out there after him, Rowan wouldn't be able to hold the circle long without her. If the circle failed, they'd all be attacked.

She'd better think of something fast.

Aedan pulled up in front of the garage and turned off the car. The interior light flicked on as he opened the door and stepped outside.

CHAPTER 22

"Rowan. Oh, God, stop and help me!" Viktoria screamed. "Stop! Aedan's in danger." Viktoria no longer cared if Rowan succeeded in learning what Niko was up to. All she cared about now was making sure Aedan stayed safe. If the shadows attacked him, they could do serious, even fatal, damage.

Aedan cleared the car and slammed the door closed. The beep of the locks engaging carried over the whispers and cries of the shadows surrounding the circle.

Viktoria dared another glance at Rowan, who had severed her lock on the crystal ball and now stood in front of the altar.

"Cut a door, Viki, and go get him. I'll hold the circle."

Viktoria ran to the south gate, the one closest to where Aedan's car had stopped. Ten metres and a host of shadows separated them. She crouched to the ground and visualized a door forming as she traced a vertical rectangular outline into the energy dome she and Rowan had created.

Sword gripped tight in her hands, she stepped through the door and sealed it behind her. She'd get him into the store, ensure his safety, and then return to help Rowan.

"Lord and Lady, help your children," she said before plunging into the darkness. "Aedan. I'm coming. Don't move. Stay quiet."

As soon as she spoke, the shadows moved on her. She swung the sword, keeping them at bay with a spray of power. The physical sword couldn't hurt them. Her energy and power were what mattered here. The sword was a conduit.

"Viktoria? What the hell's happening here?"

Oh, God, why wouldn't he listen to her and keep his mouth shut?

The shadows pivoted and descended on him.

His scream, when it came, pierced her heart.

"Aedan." Viktoria tried to run, but the air was thick, and she felt as if she moved under water. She swung the sword, focusing her energy on cutting through to Aedan.

When she reached him, he was on the ground, curled up against the car, fists pummelling the air. The shadows scraped across his body. Welts criss-crossed his arms where he'd made contact with the beings.

"Aedan, get up."

He continued to swing at the shadows.

Not knowing what else to do, she kicked him in the hip as gently as she could while making sure he felt the jolt. "Get up, damn it!"

He didn't reply, but he got to his feet. Pressed against the side of the car, Aedan appeared unable to move. He resumed flailing his arms, fighting off the shadows continuing to plague him.

Viktoria snagged one of his arms as it whizzed past her face and, sword held aloft, she dragged him away from the car. "Keep moving. To the house."

All her effort focused on slicing through the shadows. Something trickled down her arm. They'd cut her, too.

Beside her, Aedan grunted and then stumbled. She yanked him to his feet. The store loomed up in front of her, and she dragged him to the side door. She shoved him at the door. "Open it and go inside."

"No. I'm not leaving you alone with them."

"Open the fucking door! If you ignore me one more time, I'll give you to them, so help me."

He opened the door and stepped inside, but then held it open for her. "Get in here, Viki."

"I'm going back for Rowan. We have to banish them and take down the circle. Lock yourself inside. It's protected, and they don't want you." She pinned him with her gaze. "Do it. I'll be back for you, and then you'll get an explanation."

And he'd want a detailed explanation.

But so would she.

He wasn't supposed to be here. Why had he shown up exactly when it would cause them the most problems?

Viktoria turned toward the circle. Behind her, the door slammed, and the deadbolt thudded home. Thank the Goddess, he'd followed her orders this time. She didn't have time to argue with him.

Sword waving, she wrestled her way back toward the circle's south gate.

Even without Aedan to worry about, the struggle was only slightly easier. They swarmed her, sliced at her. She strengthened the psychic protection she had around herself, but they still clawed through. By the time she reached the south gate, blood dripped from scratches on her arms and legs.

Inside the circle, it was dim, murky. She couldn't see the interior but didn't have time to focus.

Viktoria cut a door again while the creatures fought to get past her. They weren't after her, either, she concluded. Their target was Rowan.

Before she could seal the door again, two of them slipped inside but burned up instantly when she thrashed them with the sword. She fell to her knees, the shock of what she'd had to endure making her weak and nauseated.

"Rowan." Viktoria stabbed the ground with her sword and leaned on it to pull herself to her feet.

When there was no response, she looked where she'd last seen Rowan. Her heart froze at the sight of Rowan lying unconscious in front of the altar. Viktoria raced over and dropped beside her friend. "Rowan, oh, God. Wake up."

Viktoria checked Rowan's pulse. It was thready but there. She patted her friend's cheek.

A noise like an incoming freight train made her look up. A funnel cloud of wind danced around outside the circle but couldn't force its way in. The shadow creatures had moved back, away from the vicinity of the ritual circle.

Whoever had sent the shadow creatures, and Viktoria was convinced it had been Niko, had pulled them back and sent this new menace. The circle strained against the onslaught of the vortex. The funnel moved counterclockwise around the circumference, and it started to suck the protective energy from around them.

Forced to leave Rowan's side, Viktoria gripped the sword and walked the circle's perimeter. She chanted, calling on the elementals and the lord and lady for help.

Air, Fire, Water, and Earth,
Lord and Lady, hear my call;
Protect all within the circle's girth,
While ye the shadows and vortex banish all;

It was the best she could come up with, under the circumstances. She walked, using the sword to increase the energy of the original circle cast. She repeated the chant, louder, faster as she increased her pace.

In her periphery, Rowan lay motionless. Worry for her friend's health and safety distracted her and made her stumble, but her chanting never wavered. "Air, Fire, Water, and Earth." She continued walking, the world outside of her circle a dark blur. She quickened her pace until she almost ran.

The power surging through her made her light on her feet, energized her.

Wind whipped and a limb broke from one of the trees shading the circle, but even that couldn't penetrate the shield she'd made. "... banish all." She finished again, her voice strong and confident.

In a vision, the Goddess matched her step for step.

The ground trembled, the force of the vortex meeting the force of the protection around the circle. A screech, like sheet metal peeling off a roof, set her teeth on edge. Viktoria kept her footing but came close to collapsing in the sand that made up the base of the circle.

As suddenly as the onslaught had come, it vanished. The night returned, and with it, the chirp of crickets and the soft whoosh of traffic from the busy street out front. Strings of fairy lights twinkled once again on the trees, and Viktoria saw no sign of the tree branch she'd heard fall.

The shadow creatures had disappeared as well, much to Viktoria's relief. She dove to Rowan's side, setting the sword on the ground beside her.

"Rowan!" A sob caught in Viktoria's throat. "Why won't you wake up?"

CHAPTER 23

No sooner did the wind die down and the shadows disappear than Aedan was outside and racing toward the circle.

He halted at the perimeter, unable to enter.

"Viki."

She looked up at him, and the fear and grief in her eyes speared terror through his chest.

"What happened to Rowan?" He tried again to step through the south gate and met resistance.

Viktoria rose and staggered to the gate. "I'll cut a door."

Aedan had no idea what that meant but waited while she performed a bizarre pantomime and waved him through.

"Do you have your phone?"

He nodded.

She held out her hand and it trembled. "Please, let me use it. I have to call for help."

Aedan snatched his cell phone from his side and passed it to her.

While she called nine-one-one, he knelt beside Rowan and checked her pulse. He had no idea what a normal heart rate was, but hers seemed fast to him. Her breath was shallow and hitched.

Viktoria knelt in the sand again and cradled Rowan's head in her lap. "If she dies, it's all my fault." Tears streamed down her face. "Help me carry her out of the circle? I need to cut a door for us."

When he agreed, she did the strange pantomime ritual with the knife she kept in a sheath on her belt. He didn't question anything, choosing to hold off until they had Rowan settled.

"Okay. We'll bring her out here onto the grass. I don't want to mess with this when the ambulance gets here."

Aedan lifted Rowan gently in his arms, Viktoria helping him. Together they set Rowan down on the grass and knelt beside her.

"What happened here, Viki?"

"Not now, Aedan. Why are you here?"

"You called me."

Her eyes went wide. "No, I didn't. Why did you come here?"

"Viktoria, I got a call from you, asking me to meet you in the circle at The Green Witch."

"What made you believe it was me?"

"The call display said 'Kovacs, V,' and I recognized your voice."

"I didn't call you."

Approaching sirens interrupted the discussion.

Aedan leaped up to meet the paramedics.

***

The doctor who came to the waiting room where Aedan, Viktoria, Mackenzie, and Terrance sat explained Rowan had a brain aneurysm and was in a coma. The aneurysm was small and hadn't ruptured, and they would monitor it, but she wasn't waking up. The doctor believed the coma was unrelated to the aneurysm.

"She might wake up tomorrow, or she might stay this way indefinitely. She doesn't need life support, which is good. We're confident it'll be a matter of time, but we can't explain why she won't wake up."

"When can I see her?" said Terrance.

"After we transfer her out of intensive care."

Terrance thanked the doctor, who assured them Rowan was in good hands and returned to his duties.

After he left, everyone turned to Viktoria, and she knew they sought answers from her she didn't want to give.

Aedan took her hands in his and raised her arms to display the bandages covering them. He lifted his own arms to show he had a matching set. "How did this happen? I was there, and I have no idea how my arms got shredded."

Viktoria winced. "I can explain." But she didn't want to.

How could he possibly believe her? Even worse, how would she prevent him from reporting on any of this?

"This isn't the place to discuss it." Viktoria scanned the room.

Five other people sat waiting for news of loved ones.

"You'll find it difficult to believe, and it's a long story."

Eyes sad, Terrance met Viktoria's gaze. "I have time. What happened to Rowan? What did this to her?"

"Terry, please. Let's take this outside."

"I'm not leaving the hospital until I verify Rowan will be okay."

Viktoria checked the time. Almost nine, and she hadn't taken down the circle. "I have to go back to The Witch. I can't leave the circle the way it is."

Terrance frowned. "Whatever you two were doing in there caused this, didn't it?"

"I'm not sure, Terry." But she squirmed under his laser-eyed stare. Perhaps performing their ritual hadn't caused the aneurysm, but she was positive it was responsible for the coma. Niko had Rowan trapped.

The digital recorder. Maybe something Rowan had said before she collapsed would help find a way to bring her out of it.

"I have to go." What if Niko knew they'd recorded the session? He could have already gone to the circle and retrieved the recorder. She backed toward the doorway. "I'll come back after I've cleaned up the circle."

Aedan raced to her side and grabbed her by the arm. "You're not going alone."

"Aedan." He was the last person she wanted along on this venture. "I've got work to do."

"Right. And I'm going with you."

"You can't help me."

"Perhaps, but you'd be crazy to go by yourself. You could get attacked." He let out a huff of frustration. "There's no point arguing with me. I'm going."

Viktoria wrenched her arm from his. "Fine. At least this way I don't have to call a cab." She turned to Terrance and Mackenzie. "Text a list to me of whatever you need, and I'll bring it when I return. I'll open the store tomorrow, Mac."

"Thanks, Vik," Mackenzie said.

"I'm so sorry, Mac, Terry. Rowan will get better. She's a fighter."

"You owe us an explanation, Viki," Terrance said. But when Viktoria opened her mouth to speak, he held up a hand. "It can wait, but you'll have to tell me soon."

"Of course."

They said their goodbyes, and with Terrance and Mackenzie's grief-stricken faces haunting her, Viktoria turned and walked from the room.

CHAPTER 24

Once they were in the car and headed toward The Green Witch, Aedan insisted on the explanation Viktoria had managed so far to avoid providing.

"I walked into the ninth circle of hell when I arrived, at, as far as I knew, your request. We're heading back to who knows what? You owe me an explanation."

"Off the record."

"The record." Lips twisted down, he gave her a sideways glance.

"You don't report any of what I tell you."

"I can't guarantee that."

"Then I won't say anything." And she didn't want him to see anything more. "Drop me off and then leave."

"Viki, the cat's out of the bag. I saw those shadow creatures—they cut me."

"Feel free to report that. It'll cause more trouble for you than it will for me. You'll turn your newspaper into a tabloid overnight."

"I'm not leaving you alone there. God knows what could come after you," he said as he pulled into The Green Witch's driveway.

"I'll be fine." She stepped from the car. "Good night. Go home and get some sleep."

Shaking his head, Aedan turned off the car and got out. "I'm not leaving until I'm sure you're safe and you've explained to me what the hell happened."

He scanned the yard, froze.

Viktoria followed his gaze.

The ground around the circle was trampled, the grass scorched. Viktoria's heart fluttered. He'd been here—Niko had come to the circle after they'd left.

She tested the strength of the energy, and it seemed solid. *Oh, please let the recorder still be there.*

Viktoria rushed to the south gate and cut a door using her athame. It occurred to her then she'd worn the ceremonial knife to the hospital and no one had noticed. Her cape probably hid it well enough.

She'd gotten curious stares at the way she was dressed, but the sheath had been tucked well into the folds of her skirts and under her cape. Thank the Goddess for small favours. She didn't want to have to explain it to hospital security. Before she returned to the hospital, she'd better change to street clothes.

That she'd been required to cut the door was a relief. It meant the protection around the circle still held. But if Niko was powerful enough, he could have cut his own door and entered.

She stepped into the circle. Aedan followed her, but she ignored him and sealed the door.

Viktoria ran to the altar and scanned it.

The digital recorder was gone.

***

"No!" Viktoria dropped to the ground and searched around the altar, hoping it had simply been knocked down when Rowan had collapsed.

"What is it?" Aedan crouched next to her.

She continued to scour the ground, using her hands to search the sand. Maybe it had gotten buried. Anything but that Niko had it in his possession. "Oh, God, no."

Aedan grabbed her by the arms and hoisted her up. "What's happening, damn it? Answer me. You owe me an explanation."

"Not if you write about any of it. Not if you insist on writing about Niko Farkas and my sister."

"This involves them." It was a statement, not a question, and she could have bitten her tongue off for having alerted him to that.

"Let me go." She struggled to throw off his grip, but he held on tight.

"What were you doing here? And why?"

"I'm not telling you. Now let go." In an instant, it hit her that the recorder was gone, and any hope she had of using what was on it to fight Niko or help Rowan had disappeared with it. Her gaze fell on Aedan's expression.

His mouth was drawn up in a grimace, his face flushed with anger. The fingers gripping her arms squeezed tight enough to cause pain. The likelihood he'd write an article that would cause her grief had increased. He didn't owe her any loyalty, and her treatment of him guaranteed he'd do it to spite her.

Hope drained out of her and despair filled the void.

Viktoria burst into tears.

"Oh, great. Not tears. Damn it. Don't." But he said it gently and released her.

When she sobbed harder and crumpled to the ground, he knelt beside her and put his arm around her. "Shh. It's okay. Whatever it is, it can't be too bad."

She thought of Rowan unconscious, maybe forever. Mackenzie without her mother. Terrance without his wife. The Green Witch without its owner. Viktoria without her best friend. Her heart ached as it had when she'd learned her sister was gone. That brought with it the reminder her sister was in the clutches of a sociopathic sorcerer.

"Oh, God, Aedan. It's worse than too bad. It's terrifying." Viktoria rocked back and forth with sobs, and then started to double over, but he caught her up in his arms.

"No, don't. What is it? Please. Tell me. Off the record. I swear, I won't print what you say without your permission."

He pressed her head onto his shoulder and held her tight against him. His cheek rested on the top of her head, and it eased the torment.

"It's Niko."

"What about him?"

"I don't know what to say. You won't believe me."

"After what I saw tonight?" He paused. "Are you saying Niko's responsible for those black things that attacked us?"

"I'm sure of it, though there's no proof."

"Why would he do that?"

"We tried to spy on him. Remotely. He's got protection around him—just as we have around the building and property here. Rowan thought if she used the crystal ball, we'd be able to work around it."

"I don't understand. You mean like fortune telling?"

"More. With the crystal ball, she could see past, present, maybe future. She focused on Niko. I saw some of it—where he came from. But then those shadow creatures attacked, and I had to hold the circle." She angled her head up so she could meet his eyes. "You showed up at the exact wrong moment."

Her breath hitched, and she had to stop talking. After a moment, she was able to continue. "I didn't call you, Aedan. He tricked you into coming here."

"Why?"

Viktoria stopped crying and rubbed the tears from her eyes. Drained, she leaned against Aedan, comforted by his solidity. "Maybe to draw me out of the circle, away from Rowan. I was protecting her."

"He used me to lure you out and attack her? How did he manage to make the call?"

She shook her head. "He's—" Viktoria couldn't say the word out loud. He'd think she was crazy.

"Tell me."

She opened her mouth, but nothing came out. How could she tell him the truth? She wasn't sure herself what it was. "I can't."

"He's what, Viki. Say it."

It would be good to tell someone. Without Rowan, she was alone in this. His eyes showed only compassion and concern. "Oh, God, Aedan, he's a sorcerer, and he's trying to hurt me."

"Why? I don't understand."

"That's the million-dollar question. That's why we were doing what we were doing." She put her head in her hands and blew out an exasperated breath. When she looked up again, their gazes locked.

She lowered her gaze and it landed on his lips.

He had a beautiful mouth. She had an urge to trace it with her finger, and it took all her self-control to keep her hands to herself. Sudden awareness she huddled in his arms brought with it self-consciousness and, reluctantly, she started to pull away.

"Wait." His hands slid up her back and kept her close. "No one will hurt you. I won't allow it."

Their gazes locked again, and this time, she saw longing.

"You fascinate me, Viktoria. I haven't been able to stop thinking about you since we met." His hands cupped her face. He dipped his head and brushed her lips lightly with his. The delicate touch sent butterflies flittering through her stomach.

Her brain fuzzed over, and when he plunged again, more fiercely, she met him with equal force. The desire she'd been supressing since the moment he'd walked into her reading room raced through her body. She circled her arms around his shoulders and clung and sampled.

His lips nipped hers and then he deepened the kiss, his arms banding around her.

"Aedan." She breathed out his name and ran her hands through his hair. For an instant, she forgot everything except that she'd finally been able to taste him. If only this moment could last forever.

Where they were now, what they were doing, and what had happened crashed together. She slipped her hands onto his chest and pushed him lightly away.

"I had to." He said it easily. "I've been wanting to do that—and more— since we met. I'm sorry. This is the worst time to indulge that urge, but I had to kiss you."

She averted her eyes. "Rowan's in the hospital."

"I know. Viki, I'll help you with whatever you need to do here, and then we'll return to the hospital and figure out the rest." He tucked a finger under her chin and raised her head, forcing her to look in his eyes once more.

Her heart thudded in her chest from a mixture of desire for Aedan and fear of Niko. "He'll come after me now. I sense it."

"Would he attack you the way he attacked Rowan?"

She shook her head. "Worse. When he comes after me, it'll be far worse." As she said the words, she recognized them to be true.

Niko had a plan for her, and whatever it was, it would be worse than a coma.

CHAPTER 25

Viktoria, a barefoot goddess, took down the circle.

Aedan didn't understand the ritual but found it fascinating. She'd asked him to stand beside the altar while she released the energy she and Rowan had raised and closed the circle.

Her slender form acquired a strength and magnificence as she walked the perimeter counter-clockwise. The swirl of energy she controlled took his breath away. Her words to the elements, to the god and goddess, enchanted Aedan.

His gaze never left her, save for the quick glances he spared when she pointed here and there. The tip of the knife she carried sparked with power. The sword and the broom, tools of the ritual, channeled the energy where she directed.

When it was done, the circle became ordinary again. A sense of loss and emptiness hit Aedan, even though the night air was warm and pleasant. The everyday world lacked the magick her circle had evoked, and Aedan was saddened by its absence.

She sheathed the ritual knife and approached him.

"You look like a warrior with that sword and knife.

"Athame, not knife."

"Looks like a knife to me."

She stood before him, her face tilted up just so. He wanted to grab her and kiss her again but didn't want to cause her uneasiness. How could she have the aura of a warrior yet appear so delicate?

Viktoria smiled. "Athames are ritual tools. I don't use mine to cut anything." She removed it from the sheath at her waist. "Still," she said and showed him the blade, "both sides are sharp enough to cut."

"And the sword?"

"Dull. I use it to cast."

"Have you completed what you wanted to do here?"

"Almost. I have to clean up the space—take down the altar, put the tools away." She walked to the east gate and stepped from the circle. From under the massive maple tree standing nearby, she picked up a large, plastic container. "Give me a hand?"

He nodded, and she returned to the circle and set the box next to the altar.

The next few moments became precious to him.

They talked, an easy patter they'd never had before. He asked her questions about the items she had on the altar, and she explained their meaning and use. Even though the protective circle was gone, the backyard was a haven.

Confused, he asked her how that could be and why Niko wasn't attacking.

"It takes energy to unleash that kind of power. He did it before because he caught us invading his privacy, but doing so depleted his energy. You can't maintain that indefinitely, but he reacted to our intrusion with force."

Aedan raised his brows, and she said, "I'm not sorry about it—we had to protect ourselves. I'm only sorry he hurt Rowan."

"Why are you so sure it was Niko?"

"Who else? We pried into his life, into his secrets. We have to find out what she learned, because he won't stop." She paused. "Most of the time, the protections Rowan has on the store and property suffice. They ward off the toxic energy and negative people who might cross our paths each day. The energy we raised in the circle protected us while we went after him."

And when Aedan had shown up, she'd had to expose them to save him. "I'm so sorry. I got that phone call and thought it was you. If I hadn't shown up when I did, maybe Rowan wouldn't be in the hospital." God, he hoped Rowan would recover quickly. He'd played a role in exposing her to harm, and that enraged him.

Viktoria took his hand. "Niko tricked you. You had no reason to suspect that wasn't me on the phone. We failed to shut him out, but I did learn one thing about him."

"What?"

"He's older than he looks."

***

Viktoria released Aedan's hand. "Come on. I've got to pack some things for the Swifts and get back to the hospital." She pointed to her car, parked next to his in the driveway. "I'll take my car. You go on home and get some sleep."

"I'm not leaving you alone here."

"The place is protected."

"Yes. From, what did you say? Ordinary toxic energy and negative people? But not from Farkas. He could come after you again."

She had no answer to that. He was right. Niko might have tired himself out, or he might have stopped because he'd won. The possibility existed he'd come back for Viktoria if she remained here alone. "Okay."

Aedan helped her go through the list and pack up a suitcase for Rowan and some food for Mackenzie and Terrance. By the time they loaded up Viktoria's car, it was close to ten o'clock.

"It's late. I'll be okay from here."

"Why are you trying to ditch me?" He frowned, annoyed. "I want to make sure you get home all right."

"I'm not a child, Aedan. I can take care of myself."

"I know. I've seen you in action. But I'd sleep better knowing you were home safe. Does your apartment have protection enough against Farkas?"

It probably didn't, but she refused to tell him that. "I'll be fine." Hopefully.

He looked uncertain for a moment and then shook his head. "No. Sorry. If you end up hurt because I let your stubborn pride dictate, I'd never forgive myself. I'll follow you to the hospital and then home. Once you're safe in your apartment, I'll head home myself. I've got to get home to my dog, anyway."

That seemed a reasonable compromise, so she accepted.

While she led the way to the hospital, she contemplated what had happened between them. They'd kissed. Rowan had been right: the sexual tension between them had been sizzling since they'd met.

He was a damn good kisser.

She touched her lips with a finger, recalling the sensation of his mouth on hers. It was kind of him to follow her to the hospital and then back to her apartment. If she wasn't careful, she'd believe he was a nice guy. Then she'd really be in trouble.

Viktoria pulled into the parking lot of the hospital, and Aedan's car glided into a space beside hers. She hopped out and opened her trunk.

They collected what they'd brought and made their way to Rowan's room. They were stopped by a nurse and had to beg to be let through, promising to keep the visit brief. Terry and Mackenzie greeted them when they entered the room. Rowan lay motionless in the bed, an IV in her arm.

Viktoria set the bag she carried on the wide windowsill. "The suitcase has your mom's stuff. The cooler bag has snacks and bottles of water for you and your dad. I found everything on this list and some extras I thought you might want."

Mackenzie hugged Viktoria. "Thank you."

"You deserve an explanation, Mac, Terry." Viktoria kept her gaze moving from one to the other as she explained what had happened. As she finished the story, she said, "Rowan was trying to help me, and now she's hurt. I'm so sorry, Mac."

"It's not your fault, Viki. Mom didn't tell me what was happening, but she worried about you. I appreciate everything you're doing for us. Dad does too." She sighed. "I had to fight with the nurses to let us both stay here tonight, but we refuse to leave. She can't be left alone."

"Don't worry about the store. I'll be in to open. Are you both taking the day off?"

"Yes," Terry replied. "We'll take turns sleeping on this chair." He pointed at it. "It folds down into what might laughably be called a bed."

She leaned over Rowan and kissed her forehead. When she straightened up, she said, "Call me if you need anything or if she wakes up."

They all hugged, but as Aedan and Viktoria turned to leave, Mackenzie called Viktoria back. Aedan stepped into the hall to wait for her.

"What is it, Mac?" Viktoria put a soothing hand on Mackenzie's arm.

"Why'd Aedan come with you?"

Viktoria shrugged, surprised at the question. "Make sure I get home okay?"

"His aura changes when he looks at you, Vik. He has the hots for you."

"Knock it off, Mac."

They both laughed then, and it released a knot in Viktoria's gut. She touched a palm to Mackenzie's face. "Take care. I love you, Mac."

"Me too, Vik."

They said goodbye, and Viktoria turned away and walked from the room. Time to head home.

***

Aedan pulled into the driveway of his home in south Newmarket. He was beat, but he knew he wouldn't be able to sleep after the night's events. He'd insisted on walking Viktoria up to her apartment unit even though she'd protested.

He'd also stolen one more kiss.

Puddles greeted him at the door and rushed outside to piddle on a tree. Aedan let the dog dance in the moonlight for a bit before calling him back into the house for the night.

"We kissed, Pud." Dog trotting behind him, Aedan made the rounds of the house and verified it was secure. He headed to his bedroom. Might as well go through the motions of going to sleep. Could be he'd manage some shut-eye before he had to get up and go to the office.

Aside from what had happened at The Green Witch to stress about, his story on Eszter would run in the morning. He was glad it was done and out of his hands now, but he worried about how Viktoria would take it. And considering she suspected Niko Farkas of attacking Rowan, how would Niko react to the story?

While Adean hadn't painted Niko or Eszter in a negative light, he had questioned their version of events.

But mostly, his mind was on Viktoria and the kiss they'd shared. "I'm positive she likes me," he told the dog. "It's just a matter of time, boy. I'll bring her to meet you real soon."

Aedan pictured her having a glass of wine in his living room, eating dinner with him in the dining room, and, best of all, sliding naked into his bed.

Puddles snorted as if he'd heard the silent fantasy unfolding in Aedan's head.

"A guy can dream, can't he?" Aedan crawled into bed and turned off the light. Yes, a guy could dream.

CHAPTER 26

Mackenzie glanced at her father, who lay on the foldout chair snoring. How he could sleep on that contraption was beyond her and also the reason she'd offered to take the first watch.

A magazine sat open but unread in her lap, the air-brushed model in the cosmetics ad staring out at Mackenzie with half-lidded eyes. Mackenzie met the gaze, and the eyes blinked.

She shook her head and examined the photo, but everything was back to normal. The room was dark, and she'd been reading by the light of the flashlight app on her cell phone. She was tired, her imagination probably playing tricks. To shake off the fatigue, she closed the magazine and went to her mother's side.

Rowan lay unmoving, one arm on the coverlet. The other arm, hooked to an intravenous drip, was hidden under the blanket. Wires from her body connected to a monitor. She wore a blood pressure cuff and had a monitor on her finger to check oxygen levels. All ran silent.

The faint rasp of Rowan's breathing reassured Mackenzie. Rowan's breath was even, settled. Was she aware her family was with her? Had she heard her husband and daughter talking to her before they finally turned off the lights and quieted down for the night?

More family would arrive in the morning. Rowan's five sisters and three brothers were expected during morning visiting hours, with other extended family trickling in over the next day or so.

Mackenzie picked up Rowan's hand and kissed it softly. "I love you, Mom," she whispered. "He won't get away with this."

Viktoria and Mackenzie had put protection around the hospital room. Hopefully, it would hold long enough to give them all a rest.

After the protections had gone up, pressure had throbbed in Mackenzie's head and behind her eyes. At the time, she hadn't told anyone, not wanting to worry her father or Viktoria. As the night wore on, the pressure had eased, so Mackenzie attributed it to stress.

Now, the tension in her head had built again. As a precaution, Mackenzie strengthened the protection around the room, on herself, and on her father. The effect on her head was minimal, so again she attributed the headache to stress.

She kissed Rowan's hand once more and set it back down on the bed. Restless, she walked to the washroom. Thank God, her dad had great medical benefits, so her mom had a private room. They wouldn't have been allowed to stay if there'd been another patient in the room, and certainly Viktoria and Aedan wouldn't have been permitted in after hours.

Mackenzie closed the bathroom door without turning on the light. A shadow moved in the mirror, and Mackenzie's heart leaped with fright. She flicked the light switch on, triggering the fan as well.

Nothing.

She'd probably seen her own reflection. Ridiculous. Of course, no one could be in here. The door to the room was closed. She'd have seen and heard anyone opening the main door, and before they could have slipped into the washroom, they'd have had to go through the room.

Mackenzie used the toilet and rinsed her face when she washed her hands. She opened the washroom door to go back to her seat and gasped. The door to Rowan's room stood open.

Mackenzie rushed to her mother's bed. Rowan lay as Mackenzie had left her, and Terrance continued to snore lightly on the foldout chair. Mackenzie touched Rowan's hand. It felt icy.

Afraid her mother was chilly, Mackenzie considered grabbing another blanket for her when she noticed the screen of the monitor hooked up to track Rowan's vital signs was dark.

Heart leaping into her throat, Mackenzie leaned into Rowan's face to check her breathing. Unable to hear any breath, Mackenzie panicked. Her gaze dropped to Rowan's chest, and she tried to see the rise and fall of it but couldn't.

Check her pulse, you idiot.

She snatched up her mother's wrist and pressed two fingers to where the pulse should be. Panic rising, she cried out to her father. "Daddy. Wake up. Please."

Terrance jumped from the chair, groggy, but automatically turned toward Rowan's bed. "What is it?"

"I can't feel Mama's pulse."

The light came on as a nurse stepped into the room. "Did one of you turn off the monitors?" Her voice was stern.

Mackenzie pointed to the silent machine. "It was off when I came out of the washroom. Please, help. She's not breathing."

The nurse glanced at the monitor. "Still set to 'on.' Maybe it shorted out." She nudged Mackenzie gently out of the way and checked Rowan's pulse.

A grim expression crossed the nurse's face, and she launched into action.

***

Aedan woke to the sound of crying and a woman sobbing out his name. Disoriented, he leaped from the bed, jostling the dog sleeping at his feet, and scanned the room.

All was silent. Must have been part of his dream, but it had seemed so real. He tried to recall the dream but couldn't.

He glanced at the time. Six in the morning. He'd had maybe four hours' sleep, but he was wide-awake now. Before anything else, he needed a piss and coffee—definitely in that order.

Aedan went into the bathroom and used the toilet, glimpsing his shadowed eyes, mussed hair, and scruffy chin in the mirror. God, he looked as rough as if he'd spent the previous night boozing and carousing.

The phone rang as he fixed his coffee. Grabbing his mug, he returned to the bedroom where he'd left his cell.

"Aedan McCarthy."

At first, there was only sobbing.

His heart raced. *Rowan.*

Before he could speak, Viktoria blurted out, "She's dead. Aedan, Rowan's dead." The last was said on a moan of despair and grief.

He wanted to ask a thousand questions but said instead, "I'm coming over, Viki. Will you be okay until I get there?"

"Yes." She choked that out through her tears.

After he hung up, Aedan let the dog outside and then rushed through getting dressed. He moved in a daze, trying to come to terms with Rowan's death. How could she have died? The prognosis hadn't been bad. Sure, she'd had an aneurysm they'd have to monitor, but she was in the hospital where she was receiving excellent care and attention.

He took the time to shave but skipped breakfast, though he filled the dog's food and water bowls.

Puddles scratched at the patio doors and gave a small bark, so Aedan let him back into the house. "I'll be back by lunch, buddy." He patted the dog's head.

The cell phone sounded again, and, heart in his throat, Aedan answered it.

"Aedan, darling, I saw the story in the paper this morning."

At first, Aedan thought it was Viktoria again. It was her voice. But then he realized it was Eszter. "Yes. Great. I'm sorry, Eszter, I was just on my way out."

He stuck his wallet in his pants pocket and grabbed his car keys off the dresser.

"Everything all right? You sound upset."

The words stuck in his throat, but he forced them out. "Rowan Swift died."

"Oh, I'm so sorry. Viktoria must be devastated. I'd better call her."

Aedan halted on his way to the door. "I'm going there right now." Should he have told Eszter? She'd no doubt tell Niko. Maybe Niko was behind Rowan's death. On the heels of that came the fear Eszter might be in danger.

"Meet me at Viktoria's."

"Why don't I come to your place, and we'll go together?" Her voice was like silk, an invitation.

She'd flirted with him when he'd interviewed her. He'd rather avoid her, but he wanted to get her away from Niko, and he needed to get to Viktoria's. "No time. Meet me there."

"All right, Aedan."

Aedan heaved a sigh of relief, disconnected the call, and left the house.

CHAPTER 27

Viktoria lay on the couch in the living room, the cell phone still in one hand. Unable to muster up the energy to lean over to the coffee table and set it down, she let it slide to the floor. It hit the carpet with a muffled thud.

Walter, her cat, picked that moment to jump onto Viktoria's stomach. She huffed out a breath and shoved him back onto the floor.

Rowan was dead.

Every time Viktoria remembered, she burst into tears, and this time was no exception. How was it possible? Rowan couldn't die—not now.

The call had come at five in the morning, jarring Viktoria out of sleep. Mackenzie was on the other end, sobbing, and Viktoria didn't need to hear the words to know why. Mackenzie had said Rowan had taken a turn during the night and had died despite the valiant efforts of the doctors to resuscitate her.

No longer having a reason to stay at the hospital, Mackenzie and Terrance were returning to The Green Witch. Mackenzie had said she'd post a note alerting customers the store was closed due to the death of the owner. "I'll take it over and reopen it in a week. I'd like to have you with me, Viki, if you want to continue there."

Of course, Viktoria had said she would.

But now, she lay on the couch, unsure how she would manage to return to the store. Rowan was dead because of her.

The tears flowed again, and she sobbed so loudly she almost missed the buzzer.

She dragged herself to the intercom and pressed the button without bothering to find out who was there. Too tired to return to the couch, she leaned against the wall and waited for the knock on the door.

Her knees shook, wobbling her legs. Each breath was too much trouble to take. It occurred to her she hadn't put up her protections, but she mentally shrugged. Who cares? Let him attack her. What did it matter?

When the knock came, she jumped even though she'd been expecting it. She swung the door open.

*****

Aedan caught her before she hit the floor. "Viki, God, what have you done?"

She groaned, the sound muffled by his shoulder. A ragdoll, she was dead weight against him. He scooped her up into his arms and carried her to the couch. What was wrong with her? It had to be more than Rowan's death. Aedan set her on her back and took her hand.

She stared at him with listless eyes. "Thanks for coming." She said the words as though each one was weighted with lead.

"Did you take pills?" Should he call nine-one-one? What if she'd overdosed? Panic erupted in his belly.

"No. Nothing. Rowan. I want Rowan."

She'd lost herself to grief. It was all he could come up with. "What happened to Rowan?"

"She died in her sleep."

"How?"

"They don't know. Her heart stopped." Her head lolled to the side. "He did it."

He understood who she meant. "How do you know?"

"I see him. When I close my eyes, he's there." She smiled. "It feels good to close my eyes."

Terrified Viktoria would lapse into a coma as Rowan had, Aedan patted her cheeks. "No, keep your eyes open. Put up protection? Tell me how." He sat beside her on the couch and hauled her into his arms. "Talk me through it. We'll do it together."

"Oh, Aedan. We got to the hospital and put up protection, but I left her. I should've and boosted her energy. It was supposed to be over. We weren't in the circle anymore. She wasn't bothering him anymore."

Niko had attacked a defenceless Rowan. Rage surged through Aedan, but with it, a measure of relief. A protection spell should shield Viktoria if her strange state was the result of Niko attacking her.

"Come on. He's hurting you. Let's put up protection. Teach me how."

"Call in Archangel Michael."

"What?" Why would a witch call on an archangel? How could she even believe in angels?

"Like this: Archangel Michael, I call to you now. Please come with your sword of light and remove any toxic and lower-vibrating energies from me and from Aedan." She leaned her head into the hollow under his neck. "I might as well clear you, too, right?"

A lump grew in Aedan's throat, and his guts tightened.

Was she drunk? He wanted to shake her, give her coffee, or take her to the hospital, but he wasn't sure which would do the trick. Safer just to let her continue with her ritual. It couldn't hurt.

She went through a process she said would create a mirror ball of protection that would only allow beneficial and loving energy in. It would deflect and transmute toxic energy.

He didn't believe any of it, but then, he'd never have believed what he'd seen in the circle the night before if he hadn't witnessed it for himself.

The buzzer buzzed.

Eszter. He'd forgotten she was on her way. Aedan eased Viktoria onto the couch and went to let in Eszter.

He unlocked the door and returned to the couch.

Viktoria had perked up and sat leaning against a couple of throw pillows.

Relieved she was returning to normal, Aedan offered to make tea and went to the kitchen. He put the kettle on as the knock sounded on the door.

"It's open," he called out and went to meet Eszter.

Eszter pushed the door open so fiercely it banged into the wall. She scanned the room and zeroed in on Viktoria. "Oh, sweetie. Sorry about your friend."

Viktoria stood, but instantly sank to the couch again. "Eszter. I'm glad you're here. I'm so tired."

Eszter rushed to her side and stared down at her. "You're pale." She turned to Aedan. "What's wrong with her?"

"She's been up most of the night. Worried about Rowan." He didn't want to mention Niko. Eszter sounded a lot like Viktoria and someone had called him last night pretending to be her.

Why Eszter would want to plot against her twin was a mystery, but she'd been with Niko for five years. He could have talked her into anything during that time.

If Eszter viewed Niko as her saviour, and based on what she'd said during the interview, she did, she might be suffering from some form of Stockholm syndrome. She might have fallen for the man who was, in reality, her captor.

Once he'd come up with the idea, it quickly gained traction for him. It made sense. A man like Niko, with wealth, looks, and power, could kidnap a young, impressionable girl like Eszter and manipulate her into believing she was now with him by choice.

But what the hell did he want with Viktoria?

CHAPTER 28

Viktoria gratefully accepted the mug of tea Aedan handed her. She cupped her hands around it, letting the hot ceramic warm her cold hands.

He smiled, and that warmed her, too.

"You're shivering." Concern laced his voice. "I'll adjust the temperature for you."

Her gaze followed him as he went to the thermostat and fiddled with it.

"How can I help, Viki?"

Viktoria turned to face Eszter. "I'm fine. I have to get dressed and go to Mac and Terry. They must be enduring hell." She studied Eszter's face.

Eszter had a rosy glow, and if you were unaware she had a fatal disease, you would believe her the picture of health. Her white dress was a stark contrast to her tanned skin. Her golden hair was smoothed back into a tight bun, and her makeup and nails were meticulously done. She'd taken the time to put herself together before coming to the apartment.

"How's Niko, Ess?" What did Eszter know of Niko's attack on Rowan? Viktoria wanted to find out but wanted to be discreet about it.

"He's fine. He was up and about early this morning—gone before I even got out of bed. Business. In Toronto."

"He's not home?" That was hard to believe, though Viktoria supposed he could have a private office from which to attack Rowan. "Did he go out last night?" Someone had gone to the circle while everyone was at the hospital.

"No. He came home exhausted, and we stayed in."

Viktoria considered. If Eszter was lying, she was in on it with him. Viktoria discarded the idea. They were twins. They loved each other. Eszter would never hurt Viktoria or her friends.

In that case, Niko was manipulating Eszter, fooling her. "Eszter, I don't trust Niko."

"That's not news to me. You've been suspicious and judgemental of him since you met him. What's your problem?"

To ease the pounding flaring up behind her temples, Viktoria sipped her tea. After a moment, she met Eszter's gaze. "He might not have your best interests at heart, Eszter." That was an understatement. Niko, she was sure, only had Niko's best interests at heart.

If he was capable of killing his own grandfather, he was capable of anything.

"Rowan and I were digging into his past when he attacked her."

"You're crazy. Niko was with me last night." Eszter spun around to Aedan. "Tell her she's crazy."

Aedan shook his head. "I'm sorry, Eszter." His gaze bounced from Eszter to Viktoria, and he hesitated, as though he wanted to say something more but couldn't.

Hesitantly, Viktoria asked, "Did you know he's a sorcerer?"

Eszter shrugged. "What of it? You're a witch."

"What do you know of his background?"

"I've met his family. I trust them. He's a good man, Viki. He would never hurt me."

"What makes you so sure he hasn't already?"

Eszter snorted. "He's kind to me. He saved my life twice. Give it a rest."

Rest. Viktoria craved some rest. But she needed to get to The Green Witch and help Terrance and Mackenzie with the funeral arrangements. That triggered tears again, and it took all her effort to restrain them.

"I have to go." Viktoria stood, and this time, she kept her feet. The pressure behind her eyes had diminished, and she breathed easier.

Aedan stood. "I'll drive you."

"No. I'll take her." Eszter took Viktoria's hand. "Don't you have work you need to do?"

Aedan hesitated and appeared to consider. "I do, but it'll wait. I've met my deadlines. My dog will need me to make an appearance at noon, but in the meantime, I'll stay with Viktoria."

"But I'm here. She's safe with me, darling."

The pressure in Viktoria's head increased, and she winced. She closed her eyes to shut out the light, which had suddenly become too bright. Fatigue threatened to overwhelm her. Images of Niko flashed through her mind's eye, but when she tried to glimpse his mind, she encountered a barrier of darkness. How many times did she have to clear and protect herself before he'd leave her alone?

When she opened her eyes again, Aedan and Eszter were both staring at her.

"I'll get dressed and go. You can both come along or not."

Viktoria turned on her heel and left the room.

***

When they arrived at The Green Witch, Viktoria led Eszter and Aedan around to the back door. Without knocking, she ushered them inside to the kitchen and called out to Mackenzie and Terrance.

Mackenzie strode into the room. Her eyes were red-rimmed and bloodshot, her hair mussed, and her clothes the same ones she'd worn the day before.

Viktoria folded the young woman into her arms and kissed her cheek. "Oh, Mac, I'm so sorry. How's your dad?"

"Devastated. I'm afraid it'll kill him. They were married for twenty-five years, Vik. He can't live without her. She was his world." Sobs wracked Mackenzie's body.

"How may we help you?" Aedan stepped forward and rested a hand on Mackenzie's arm.

"Yes, we're here to help." Eszter said. She walked around to stand behind Mackenzie and met Viktoria's gaze over the woman's shoulder.

"I have to go with Dad to the funeral home and make arrangements. But I also want to have a pagan ceremony here." Mackenzie disengaged from Viktoria's arms and raised her chin. "I'd be honoured, Viki, if you'd organize that for us."

"Of course, sweetie. I'd be proud to do it." Warmth flooded her heart. She could do this for Rowan. For Mackenzie. For Terrance. Most of all, for herself.

***

In the days following, Viktoria focused on saying goodbye to her beloved friend. With Eszter by her side, she pushed through the emotional pain and physical exhaustion, and the attacks from Niko eased up. Perhaps with Rowan gone, he no longer felt threatened.

Aedan participated in the ceremonies, including the small, private pagan ritual Viktoria led. Rowan's body was cremated according to her wishes, and the urn was placed on the altar during the ceremony.

They had a potluck afterward and reminisced about Rowan's life and what her friendship had meant to them. She'd been a role model for Viktoria, and the loss left a hole in her heart she believed would never heal.

Viktoria's parents both attended, lending their support to their daughter and their daughter's friends.

After the last guest had said goodbye, Viktoria began the cleanup of the circle, yard, and house. She'd ordered Mackenzie and Terrance up to the apartment, insisting she'd take care of everything. Staying busy would help her cope.

Without a word, Aedan had remained behind to help.

Eszter had not attended the ceremony. Her health had suffered a downturn, and she was at home, resting. Eszter's spirit was preparing to leave, Viktoria sensed, and so her heart was extra heavy as she went about packing up the ritual items.

"Where should I start?"

Aedan's shadow fell across Viktoria as she knelt before the altar and carefully wrapped a statue of the goddess in a silk cloth.

She glanced up and the sight of him soothed her aching heart. Viktoria smiled. "The kitchen. Dishes."

He knelt and took her hands in his. "You've worked so hard these past few days. The ceremony was beautiful. It was like she was here, watching."

"She was, Aedan. No doubt. And he was not."

It was true. Viktoria had enlisted Mackenzie's help and that of the other members of their group who'd be present during the pagan funeral rite. They'd ensured that only those invited into the circle showed up. Niko's energy had not tainted the ritual.

She'd felt Rowan's presence throughout the ceremony, and it had strengthened Viktoria's energy. Love had poured into the circle, and Rowan had been the source.

Viktoria and Aedan knelt together for a moment, hands held. The silence strung out between them until Viktoria finally broke it. "Thank you for staying to help me clean up."

He smiled, and when it reached his eyes, she melted inside.

"I'm happy to do it. To be honest, I've been anxious to get you alone. This has been a difficult time for all of us. We could spend the evening together."

His suggestion brought a flood of desire for normalcy and companionship. Viktoria didn't hesitate. "I'd love to. What would you like to do?"

"I'd like you to meet my dog. He's heard so much about you."

"Okay. But he's got the advantage. I haven't heard much about him. I don't even know his name."

"Puddles. He comes by it honestly."

Viktoria laughed and a world of worry dropped away.

CHAPTER 29

The sun was close to setting by the time they reached Aedan's house.

A red brick bungalow on a large lot in south Newmarket, it was quaint rather than extravagant. The lawn was green and weed free. Bushes lined the width of the house. A tree stood at attention near the road, the branches almost reaching the hydro lines.

Viktoria got the impression the house was cared for but not well loved. It was a place for Aedan to hang his hat and do his work.

When they stepped from the car, he hurried to her side and took her hand. The warmth of his palm against hers comforted, and she gave his hand a squeeze.

He opened the front door, and Puddles leaped out, dancing around them. As soon as the dog spotted Viktoria, he ran to her and would have jumped up, but Aedan ordered him to sit. "Ignore him until we're settled. I'm trying to teach him not to greet people with so much exuberance. Not everyone appreciates it."

Viktoria laughed. The dog's excitement was catching, and she had an urge to jump and dance along with him.

"He's beautiful." She did as instructed and didn't reward the dog with a pat on the head or coos of affection. But as she passed Puddles, she telepathically told him she'd give him hugs and kisses inside if he behaved.

Puddles nudged her with his snout and sedately led them into the house.

The inside was as austere and practical as the outside. No paintings adorned the neutral walls, no knickknacks cluttered the assembly-required furniture. It was clean and efficient, and without the dog, she would have found it cold.

"You must travel a lot," she said.

"Yes. Part of the job. I'm staying put for a while to write my novel. It'll make Puddles happy. He likes it when my cousin housesits, but he prefers me to stay home. I gave the paper my notice two weeks ago. They weren't thrilled, but what could they do? My mind's made up."

"Aren't you writing the novel in your spare time?"

He chuckled. "I discovered I suck at multi-tasking—at least when it comes to the book. All I want to do is work on it."

She frowned. "You haven't had much opportunity lately. I'm sorry."

"It's not your fault." He motioned for her to follow him and led the way to the kitchen.

It had the same air of sparseness. The counters were devoid of the small appliances Viktoria kept on her counters: the toaster oven, microwave, indoor grill, and juicer—compared to Aedan, she was a packrat.

"Wine?"

She wasn't driving—she'd be taking a cab home regardless of how much she drank. The prospect of sharing a quiet evening sipping wine with Aedan helped ease the steady thrum of grief that had dogged her since Rowan had died.

"Sure," she said.

He opened a wine fridge and took out a bottle of white. "I have red if you prefer. In the summer, I tend to drink more white."

"That's fine." The cool drink would be refreshing.

He poured them each a glass and suggested they sit on the patio in the backyard.

Whatever the inside of the house lacked, Aedan had poured into the yard.

Viktoria stepped into a lush garden filled with flowering plants, a small pond with running fountain, and a hot tub under a gazebo at the end of the large deck. From the deck, a cobblestone path wound through landscaped flowerbeds, through an arbour, and down to a bench next to small fishpond.

"It's charming."

"Thanks. I paid someone to do this. I have a black thumb, but I needed an oasis." He angled his head so their gazes met. "I work out here often. Have a seat." Aedan motioned her to a padded chair next to a round, glass table. The umbrella in the centre was closed, but he opened it up and plugged in the string of tiny lights. He took a barbeque lighter from a bin beside the house and made his way around the perimeter of the deck setting lanterns alight.

The effect was a cozy, twinkling space that made Viktoria feel both safe and comfortable. "I love this." She sipped on her wine, savouring the slightly sweet and fruity taste.

"Yeah, it's not a bad wine."

She laughed. "The garden. It's wonderful." She inhaled the warm night air, letting it flow into her abdomen. "I almost believe we'll have peace."

"We will." He reached across the table and took her hand. "He won't intrude here. Not tonight. Not ever. I've learned how to put up my own protections."

"Eszter is still with him." The knot in Viktoria's stomach returned. "My parents won't interfere. They're not usually fooled by someone like Niko, but they're oblivious now."

"Perhaps they're letting Eszter decide what's right for her."

"Even if she's being brainwashed?" Viktoria scoffed. "What parent would do that?"

"You believe she's been brainwashed?"

"Yes. Don't you?"

His hand slid from hers. He picked up his glass of wine and fiddled with the stem.

When the silence stretched, she broke it. "You don't want to say yes because you don't agree with me."

Aedan glanced away, uncomfortable. Finally, he faced her and said, "You're right. I doubt she's been brainwashed. Seems to me she's doing whatever the hell she wants."

"What has she done to make you believe he's not influencing her?"

He shrugged. "My impression from the interview I did with her and my observations. We've spent time together. Seems to me, no one tells her what to do."

"No. And that's another problem." Viktoria fell silent. "She's not herself, Aedan."

"What do you mean?"

"Her personality. It's not her—not how she used to be." It was so hard to explain. "When I'm with her, we clash. We used to be on the same wavelength. We're twins. I used to be able to tap into her, and she could tap into me whenever we wanted."

Viktoria stood and paced the deck. "Ever since she vanished, I lost my connection to her, and I never got it back." She swung around to face him and strode up to his chair. "I should have." The despair in her voice rang out.

Aedan took her hands in his. "Come here."

He pulled her toward him and drew her into his lap.

Automatically, she leaned into him and rested her head on his shoulder. His arms went around her. It felt natural to be here, in his yard, in his arms with his dog lying at their feet.

"A lot changes in five years. When Eszter disappeared, she was still maturing. Now, she's an adult, a woman. Whatever she endured while she was gone made her what she is today," Aedan said.

"Yes, I agree, but I don't think you mean it the way I do."

"Viki, for tonight, don't worry about Eszter, about Niko. I want to make this night about you. About us."

She shifted so she could look into his eyes. Flutters in her abdomen and a constriction in her throat made breathing difficult. His hand stroked her hair, his other arm still looped around her waist.

"Did you bring me here to seduce me?"

"Is it working?"

Softly, she said, "Yes."

"Then yes, I did." With one finger, he smoothed a lock of hair from her face and tucked it behind her ear. "I've been attracted to you from the day we met, Viki. I think you feel the same way about me. At first, I didn't want to act on it. But what I learned from that funeral rite we had for Rowan is that life is fleeting and unpredictable. If I don't tell you now, I may lose my chance."

He leaned over and kissed her lightly on the lips. With his tongue, he probed, gently. When he pulled back, he said, "It's more than an attraction, Viki. I want to say love, but we've only known each other a short time, and when we're together, emotions are high. But I want you, I care for you, and I hate being apart from you. If that's not love, it's headed there."

Aedan pulled her face to his, pressed his lips to hers, and gave her another taste. Electricity crackled between them.

All she wanted to do was drink him in and offer herself to him in return. "Yes."

The word slipped out, and in its utterance, she agreed to everything, even for what he hadn't asked.

He rose, lifting her to her feet. "Let me make love to you." His words implied gentleness, but his tone implied a wanton wildness and rough passion. "Say you want that too."

Viktoria swallowed, unable to articulate how badly she needed him inside her. "Yes, I want that."

His muscles bulged as he lifted her into his arms and carried her to the patio door.

Viktoria wrenched it open herself, suddenly anxious to get inside where she could tear off his clothes. When he stepped into the house and nudged the door closed, she gasped, "Put me down."

He did, and she took his hand and yanked. "This way's faster."

They raced to his room, Viktoria only hesitating before the closed doors because she didn't know the way. Aedan burst through the door ahead of her, his hand still clutching hers. In a frenzy of need, they stopped just inside the room and locked onto each other.

Aedan's hands grasped Viktoria's face and held it while he pressed their lips together. In a heady haze, she ran her palms over his arms and across his back. She hugged him against her and his hardness pressed against her belly.

"The bed." She gasped it and moved her hands around to tug at his shirt. Her fingers struggled to undo the buttons, and she almost tore them off. When she'd succeeded, and the shirt lay discarded on the floor, she feathered her fingers over his soft skin. He moaned, and she rose on her toes to trail kisses along his neck and chest while her hands turned their attention to getting his pants open.

"The bed." Aedan scooped her up before she could finish.

In a tangle of limbs, they hit the mattress, and he tugged the straps of her sundress from her shoulders. The strapless bra came off next, and he dove down to tongue her nipples.

Viktoria almost screamed with the unbearable pleasure. She ran her hands through his hair and arched into him.

"You taste so good," he said and devoured her mouth again.

He slid her dress down over her hips, and it joined his shirt on the floor. When only her panties remained, he kissed his way down to the thin material and explored beneath it with his fingers.

"Oh, God. Aedan. Aedan." She was empty, hollow, and she needed him to fill her up. In a daze, she heard his zipper glide down and the rustle of pants and underwear being removed and tossed to the floor. A wrapper crinkled as he opened a condom and put it on.

She focused her gaze on him, and her pulse raced at the sight of his nakedness. His hard, rangy body spiked her desire. Was it possible to lose your mind with lust? Never had she been this close to finding out. She slid her panties down and opened herself to him.

He used his fingers and tongue to send her rocketing up and then over the edge.

This time she did scream, her eyes rolling back, her body going limp as the strength drained from her.

"Now, in me, now, please." She had to have him. If he didn't enter her now, she'd never survive.

He obliged, sliding into her with a moan of delight. His body covered hers, his lips fed on hers, and his hands held hers in a perfect symphony of movement. Their rhythms synchronized, and for the first time in her life, Viktoria knew what it was to surrender to a man.

Never had she let herself go so completely. Never had she trusted so completely. He sped up, making her rise to that wild peak again. When she cried out his name, once and again, he shuddered in his release and called to her in return.

He collapsed, and they tangled together in a relaxing, sweaty embrace. When he rolled away, pulling out of her, she slung an arm and a leg across him, claiming him. She snuggled into the crook of his arm, her head on his shoulder.

Aedan kissed her forehead. "Stay here tonight."

"Walter won't like it."

"Walter?" His voice contained a hint of pique.

She laughed. "My cat. He hates it when I don't come home."

"Does he have enough food and water?"

"Yes. I gave him extra of both before I left for the funeral rite in case Mac and Terrance needed me to stay late. But I was expecting to return before morning."

"Cats aren't like dogs, right? You can leave them overnight as long as they have food, water, and a litter box?"

"Yes, but that's not the problem. Walter gets lonely if I'm not home." She propped herself up on her elbow. "I'll tell him I'll be home for breakfast. He should be okay with that."

Aedan curved his mouth up in a half-smile. "You going to phone him?"

"Ha, ha. No." She pulled the sheet up to her chin, shivering a little as the heat from the physical exertion dissipated. "I'll connect to him telepathically."

"I do believe you will." He pulled her head down for another long, sultry kiss.

CHAPTER 30

Without disturbing Aedan, Viktoria slipped out of his bed at five in the morning and, by the light of the clock radio, hunted up her clothes. Reluctant to leave without saying goodbye, she stood beside his side of the bed and watched him sleep.

His bangs drooped over his forehead, and the stubbles on his chin and cheeks made her want to climb back in and rouse him seductively from sleep. But she had to get home to Walter.

She had no idea how the day would unfold. The store was closed until the following week. Viktoria had nowhere she had to be. Despite that, time pressed her and compelled her to leave, and it was about more than just her cat.

As she let herself out of Aedan's house to wait for the cab, she turned toward the sunrise. Orange and gold light blended with the stripes of clouds across the sky. Her heart ached. Rowan would never see the sun rise again.

She gave her head a shake. Rowan could visit the earth plane and see anything she wanted. This melancholy that had settled over Viktoria since Rowan's death needed to go. It wouldn't bring Rowan back and would only open Viktoria up wider to attack. A happy, healthy attitude bolstered the protective energy she'd put around herself. Negative thoughts only shredded it.

A slight mist clouded the road in the distance. Dew glistened on the grass. Sadness overtook her despite her good intentions, and her sobs competed with the birdsong.

The night she'd spent with Aedan seemed a lovely and distant dream.

The cab arrived, and as soon as she stepped into it, the familiar pressure built in her temples, and pain punched her stomach.

Twenty minutes later, she was back in her apartment, lying on the couch, Walter curled up on her stomach. His warm body helped ease the ache.

She made an attempt to clear and protect herself, and it helped a little, but she knew she was losing the battle—and the war. As the throbbing in her head increased, it occurred to her she should have kissed Aedan goodbye. Fatigue and despair swept over her.

Her life had been so short, and now it would end. It didn't matter. Nothing mattered.

The apartment door opening made her open her eyes, expecting to see the landlord. No one else had a key to her apartment, but she didn't understand why he'd want to let himself in at this early hour.

Walter hissed and jumped from the couch. He crouched next to her on the floor, and a low growl rumbled from his throat.

Viktoria tried to sit up but found she didn't have the strength. When Niko stepped into her field of vision, she was unsurprised.

"You may stand."

Her brain remained in a fog, but her body obeyed his command.

Walter launched himself at Niko's leg, hissing and clawing. With a flick of his hand, Niko flung the cat against the wall.

Spittle flying from his mouth, Walter yowled and screamed, a high-pitched wail that had chills racing up Viktoria's spine. Unable to move, she watched her beloved pet struggle to get up from the floor to help her.

Another flick of Niko's wrist pinned the cat to the floor, and he closed his eyes and fell silent.

Inside, Viktoria struggled to fight off the control Niko had over her. It was like a stone wall around her. Under the strain and frustration, her eyes welled up with tears. He'd take her away just as he had Eszter. Maybe Aedan would become suspicious if she disappeared, but would the police believe him if he told them a pillar of the community had kidnapped her?

Desperate to find help, she sent a panicked plea to Puddles. Maybe the dog could alert Aedan that something was wrong.

Niko grasped Viktoria's elbow and ushered her out of the apartment.

***

Aedan awoke when the front door closed, but by the time he roused himself enough to get out of bed, Viktoria was gone. Her absence was a void. She hadn't even said goodbye. Uttering a frustrated curse, he turned and went to use the washroom.

He realized Puddles wasn't pestering him for food, water, and to go outside. Aedan searched for the dog and found him leaving nose prints on the patio door and raising a paw to be let back inside.

Viktoria must have let him out before she left.

"Hey, boy. Did she feed you, too?" Aedan led the dog to the kitchen and checked the bowls. As he'd half-expected, the evidence showed she'd taken care of that chore, too. "Not that you're a chore, buddy," he reassured Puddles. "But it was thoughtful of her to feed you for me, wasn't it?"

The dog wagged his tail and barked. He then spun around, chasing his tail for three spins, and curled up on the doggie bed.

Aedan considered calling Viktoria, but when the clock showed it wasn't even six yet, he changed his mind. She might have gone home to crawl back into bed. He contemplated doing the same but when he returned to his room, it was to get dressed.

He was just finishing his morning cup of coffee when Puddles leaped to his feet, growling ferociously.

Startled, Aedan rushed to the dog, who continued to snarl at nothing.

"What is it, Pud?" Aedan had never seen his dog this worked up. Sweat broke out on the back of Aedan's neck. "Puddles, what is it?"

Puddles crouched low and then lunged for the front door. He clawed at it, barking and growling.

Aedan rushed to the door and opened it.

The dog tore outside and ran to the car. He whined and pawed at the passenger door.

Viktoria.

It hit Aedan she was able to communicate with animals. She'd told him as much last night when he'd asked her to stay over. He hadn't taken her seriously, but why else would Puddles be this agitated?

This wasn't about a car ride to the dog park. Viktoria needed help.

Aedan grabbed his wallet and keys and raced back to the car. With no idea where he was supposed to go, he hesitated at the end of his driveway.

Next to him, the dog struck up a chorus of whining and barking.

"Stop," Aedan yelled. He couldn't think with all that noise. If he thought it through, he might be able to figure out where the damn dog wanted him to go.

Aedan pulled onto the road and drove toward Viktoria's apartment building.

CHAPTER 31

Viktoria shuddered to wakefulness. The room was dim, and she lay on a padded surface, her wrists and ankles secured with soft, sturdy cuffs.

She tugged on her arms and found no slack. Heart thudding, she turned her head, trying to scan her surroundings.

On her left, Eszter lay on an examination table almost close enough to touch if Viktoria's hands were free. A blanket was draped over Eszter. Her arms were exposed, and her wrists were unbound, but she was hooked up to an IV drip. Eszter's gaze met Viktoria's. The ice in her sister's eyes had fear clawing through Viktoria's body.

"Eszter," Viktoria whispered.

Eszter turned her face away and called out. "She's awake, Niko, darling."

With a whimper that shamed her, Viktoria said, "Eszter, what are you doing? Help me, please."

Footsteps approached, and Viktoria tried to whirl her head around to see who was coming though she sensed well enough it was Niko. When he entered her field of vision, it took all her self-control not to scream without stopping.

Niko wore a long, hooded cloak the colour of death. He carried a sword, and Viktoria knew the blade on this one was sharp and strong enough to cut through bone. It glinted in the light thrown off by the overhead lights.

He ignored Viktoria and went to Eszter. "My darling. Soon you'll be strong again." He leaned over her, and they kissed, Eszter moaning with pleasure when he ran his palm over her breasts.

"Make it quick, baby. I want her body now."

Viktoria's terror ratcheted up another notch at the words, but she remained silent, watching, eyes wide.

"Patience, dear one. It won't be long now." He turned his attention to Viktoria then.

Breath heaving in staccato bursts, Viktoria called on Archangel Michael to help her and sent another frantic message to Puddles. In return, she caught an image of Aedan, standing in her apartment with the landlord, who'd let him in.

Oh, God, they wouldn't realize where she was—not in time to save her. She had to somehow buy time until he found her.

She swallowed her fear and forced herself to speak with confidence. "What am I doing here, Niko? Planning to brainwash me as you did Eszter?"

Niko leaned in close to her face.

For a kiss? She shuddered.

"No, my dear. Your Eszter died five years ago," he said, his voice low, soft.

Viktoria trembled. "I don't understand." Tears sprang to her eyes. Angry at her own weakness, she bit her lip to control them.

"That's okay." He patted her arm. "You don't need to understand to help us out. Your only function now is to die."

She struggled, uselessly, and when he bent close to her again, she spit in his face.

He struck her, a ringing slap across the face.

She spit at him again, but he had moved away and it missed him.

"Don't bruise her, Niko." Eszter's voice was sharp. "I'd rather not have to deal with the results of your inability to control your anger."

"Talitha, die quietly, please." Niko lay the sword, vertically, along Viktoria's body. The point rested under her chin.

She moaned, unable to keep her fear from spilling out.

Eszter chuckled. "You're cruel, darling, but you make me laugh. Entertain me, sweetheart, until the time comes. Tell our guest what's happening. I want her to know. I want to look in her eyes and see the awareness of what's to come."

"Ah, sweet Talitha. You call me cruel, but you insist on tormenting these poor souls." He drew close to Viktoria again but kept his face away from hers. "Let me tell you a story," he said.

And he did, his voice strong with pride and passion. Some of it she already knew, such as his rise to power over the bodies of his enemies, including that of his grandfather. "He refused to join me. We could have done so much together. Our blood is strong, invincible."

Niko shook his head, sorrow and regret in his eyes. But the regret was for his grandfather's refusal to help Niko and not for Niko's murderous rage. "I will never grow old and never die. When I need a new body, I select from the best."

He caught Viktoria's face in a brutal grip, his fingers digging into her cheeks. Viktoria tried to turn her head, but he held her fast.

"Soon, my pet, you'll discover what it's like to leave your body. You'll be free. Won't it be a relief? No more cares." He released her as tears sprang to her eyes.

"If you believed that, you'd allow yourself to grow old and die, you hypocrite. Aedan knows what you are. He'll stop you."

"You knew what I was. So did Rowan. Neither of you could stop me." His eyes darkened. "I'd punish you for the inconvenience you caused, but my dear Talitha deserves to receive unmarred merchandise."

"Rowan." Viktoria's breath hitched.

"Tell her about Eszter, darling." Talitha's voice was weak and tired but held anticipation and delight.

Niko smiled indulgently at Talitha. "All right, my sweet."

***

After a fruitless search of Viktoria's apartment, which had involved coercing Mr. Ingram, the landlord, to open the door with his master key, Aedan returned to the car.

Puddles had become increasingly agitated in Viktoria's apartment, barking and pestering Aedan to leave. Ingram hadn't appreciated the dog in the apartment either, and had hounded Aedan about it. When they found Walter injured, Aedan's anxiety spiked higher. Ingram promised to take the cat to the veterinarian, but they found nothing to explain what had happened to Viktoria.

Frustrated, Aedan sat in the car with no clear idea of what to do next. What was worse, Puddles seemed to know, but Aedan had no way to find out.

But he knew who might.

Relieved to have a plan, Aedan turned left from Davis Drive onto Leslie Street and headed for The Green Witch. On the way, he punched speed dial to get Mackenzie and told her they were coming.

She was waiting outside when he pulled up.

"Don't get out of the car," she said when he opened his door.

She raced around to the passenger side and jumped in.

Puddles stuck his head into her face, and Mackenzie laughed, the sound incongruous in the fear-laced atmosphere.

"I love you, doggy," she said.

"Where are we going?" Aedan pulled onto Leslie Street and headed south toward Davis Drive.

"You know where Niko and Eszter live?"

"Yeah. Okay." Somehow he'd expected they'd end up there.

"I've called the police, Aedan. I spoke to that cop, Baker, who was investigating Eszter's disappearance. He doubted at first that Niko could have kidnapped Viktoria, but I convinced him to investigate. He's on his way there."

That reduced some of Aedan's uneasiness, but he still punched the car over the speed limit. When he rounded onto Davis Drive and headed east, he sped up even more. Let the cops try to stop him. He could use the backup—as long as Viktoria was with Niko. Aedan was positive Niko had her, but he was leading police out there. He'd better be right.

"How did you find her?"

"I asked my mother."

The car swerved as Aedan startled at the words.

"Easy there, speed racer," Mackenzie said and put a hand on his shoulder. "Did you believe my mother was truly gone? She's in the spirit world, which means I can connect to her. She visited me."

"Rowan told you where to find Viki?" Talking kept the terror at bay as well as helped him understand what was happening. As long as he could focus on anything other than what might be happening to Viktoria, he'd be okay.

"No. Puddles did. I connected with him after you called me to tell me he knew where Viktoria was. As far as my mother is concerned, it's been difficult for her to get through Niko's defences. He's powerful. But his power doesn't extend to the other side. The game changed when my mother died."

Aedan glanced at Mackenzie. Her expression was grim but determined. "He can't hold her off when she's in the spirit world. He can block me from hearing her, but he can't spread his attention too thin or he'll lose control."

"So when he focused on Viktoria and me, he let his guard down enough for you to hear from Rowan?"

"Yes. The protection we have around The Witch helps to mess him up, too. Aedan, that's not Eszter in Eszter's body."

Aedan's heart leaped into his throat. "Then who is it?"

"She's Niko's lover. Her name is Talitha."

"Talitha. Why does that sound familiar?"

"He calls her that because of what she is. *Talitha koum* is a phrase from *The Bible*. Jesus said it to a young girl he raised from the dead. It means 'little girl, arise.' Talitha is a walk-in."

His stomach sinking, Aedan asked, "What's a walk-in?"

"The sweet, new age version of it is a spirit who contracts to take over a body in which the soul wants out. So, for example, a person who has always felt they were never meant to be born and wants to return to the spirit world without going through the dying process. Someone who came here before his or her time lives in constant despair. A soul from the spirit world offers to take that person's place. One soul leaves the body, and the other one comes in."

"Then why is there suicide?"

"Walk-ins don't contract to trade with people who have lessons to learn. They only take over from people who weren't meant to be here, who weren't meant to be born. Killing yourself isn't an option, and the soul recognizes that. It lowers your spirit's vibration, sets your soul's growth back."

"Then why do some people kill themselves? And how can someone be born accidently before their time? If God is perfect, why the errors?"

"People kill themselves for many reasons. In those cases, they're not damned, but they aren't relieved of the problems that got them to that point. In the case of souls born out of turn, you're assuming it was God's mistake. Whether you believe in God or not, this has nothing to do with him, except perhaps as part of that soul's journey."

"Are you saying Eszter wasn't meant to be here?"

"No. What I told you is the accepted definition of what a walk-in is. Niko and Talitha have corrupted it. They're manipulating souls, pushing them from their bodies to take them over."

"Why?" Even as he asked, he knew and answered his own question. "Immortality. They want to live forever, and this allows them to do it." His grip tightened on the steering wheel until his knuckles turned white. "Bastard. Fucking bastard. He's killing young women so his lover can take over their bodies."

"Aedan, there's more. He's doing the same with young men—and he has his sights set on you."

CHAPTER 32

"Eszter caught my eye during her time at university. I influenced her to head to Toronto on a bus rather than wait for her boyfriend to drive her. When she stopped in Toronto, we took her." Niko put a hand on Viktoria's thigh, and she was powerless to shake it off.

"You kidnapped her. She didn't run away." She wanted to hit him. Frustration at her impotence made her scream. "You bastard!" Tears flowed from the corners of her eyes and dribbled into her hair.

"Yes. The story about rescuing her from two attackers was, of course, a falsehood. But it made me heroic, didn't it?" He didn't pause long enough for her to respond. "I brought her here. Talitha lured her to the car and we snatched her."

He glanced at Talitha. "She had a different host body then, of course. A beautiful redhead with fiery eyes. I enjoy the variety. When they reach their forties, we trade up to a newer model. It was time to find a new host when we spotted Eszter, and Talitha wanted that body. It was so fit and sexy. We imagined doing all manner of things to her." His voice turned wistful as he reminisced.

Niko ran his hand up Viktoria's thigh and pressed it against her crotch. "I've been fantasizing about what I'll do with your body, too. It'll give me years of pleasure."

Viktoria wailed in despair and struggled against the bindings.

"Talitha and I met so long ago, but our love has remained strong." Niko paused and stroked Eszter's hair. "We shared a common mind, and she helped me increase my holdings."

"He saved me. That's true enough. My father would've married me to one of his feeble old friends. But Niko made me his." Eszter turned an adoring gaze on Niko. "He carried me to his home and promised to care for me forever, and he's kept that promise."

"You didn't need rescuing. Your brother did when you murdered him."

"Niko, she was peeking." Eszter pouted. "That spoiled the story."

"Oh, God. You're both monsters," Viktoria replied.

"I'll trade in my old body soon too. Would you like to know whom I've selected for the honour of hosting my soul?" Niko said.

Understanding hit her in a sledgehammer of fear. "Oh, God."

"Yes, my dear. Your journalist has everything I want in a host body."

"You can't have his body. What would you do, become a journalist?"

He chuckled. "You amuse me. No. When I take him over, I'll travel back as Aedan McCarthy, along with Talitha in your body, to our homeland. There, I'll become a member of the Farkas family once again. It's easy enough to forge the documentation. I always return to my family. The body I'm using doesn't make me a Farkas—my soul does."

"Your soul makes you an asshole."

He laughed, long and hearty, filling the room with his sick joy. "Sometimes I wish I could keep you both. Twins would be a fun distraction. But my darling Talitha needs your body, so you'll have to vacate." He motioned toward Eszter. "She's growing weaker. The life force flows out of her."

"You have a business here. You're in the public eye. How do you think you'll get away with this?"

"Niko will disappear. They may hunt for him all they like. If they find the old body I've discarded, what does it matter? They'll declare me dead and the case closed." He grinned. "My new body will provide me with a clean slate."

He pressed the point of the sword into Viktoria's chin and, with his fingers, wiped at the blood, which he smeared onto Talitha's lips.

She suckled on his fingers, sighing with pleasure. "A wonderful story, darling. Is it time yet for my happy ending?"

"No. Please. No." Viktoria hated herself for begging—knew it was useless—but terror crumbled her self-control, and she let the words tumble out. "Please, don't. No, God, please."

"Shh. It'll all be finished soon." He gestured toward Talitha. "See how her breathing slows? The painkillers failed her. She suffered so. I gave her more to ease her pain, but they're speeding her to the end of her life."

Viktoria screamed as he turned his gaze back to her.

"Time's up." Niko set the sword on the floor, pressed his palms onto Viktoria's chest, and inside, her heartbeat slowed.

***

Aedan pulled into the driveway of the Farkas estate. Baker's vehicle was already there, and he was banging on the front door of the house. Two uniformed officers accompanied him.

As soon as the car doors opened, Puddles raced to the front door, barking furiously.

Baker turned on them, pulling his gun as he spun around. "Ms. Swift?"

"Yes," Mackenzie replied. "Hurry. Please."

The dog's panic increased and Mackenzie paled. "He's killing her. Oh, God, we've got to get in there."

Baker hesitated for only a second before he kicked the door. It shuddered but didn't open. He drew his leg back to try again.

***

Darkness pressed in on Viktoria as her vision faded. Panic drained from her in an instant, and she found herself above the scene.

Niko's hands remained on her chest, his eyes slits, and his focus on her heart. Talitha's eyes stared up, vacant and unseeing. Her spirit hovered nearby, braced to leap into Viktoria's body the moment Niko released his telepathic grip on her heart.

Neither Niko nor Talitha paid any attention to Viktoria. Either they didn't see her, or they didn't care she was still there. For a moment, they all hung, suspended in an instant of time.

Confused, unsure how to prevent the inevitable, Viktoria simply observed.

The moment shattered with the sound of smashing wood and the patter of footsteps from the ceiling above. The noise jarred Viktoria out of her confusion.

She tried to return to her body. A silver cord connected her to it, and she knew that as long as the cord remained, she could return and Talitha couldn't enter it. But the instant she thudded into her body, the airlessness and darkness seized her, and she was forced out again.

To her horror, the silver cord snapped this time, and immediately, Talitha descended toward Viktoria's body. Niko stepped back, signalling to the walk-in that the body was hers for the taking.

A ball of light intercepted, and Talitha spun away from Viktoria's body. Viktoria recognized Rowan's energy, but before she could distract herself with the joy of her friend's return, Rowan's voice cut through to Viktoria. "It's not your time, Viki. Return now."

No sooner did Viktoria think about getting back to her body than she slammed into it and found herself gasping for air. Her body arched as she fought for breath, her throat searing with the effort.

"Talitha." Niko began to remove the restraints. "Darling, I'm here."

Viktoria's eyes snapped open, and as soon as their gazes locked, he knew.

"Talitha!" This time, his hands wrapped around Viktoria's neck, and the agonizing battle for her life resumed.

The struggle lasted no more than a second. Still conscious when Niko's hands wrenched from her throat, Viktoria gasped for air.

Aedan appeared at her side, and Mackenzie was right behind him. Detective Baker held Niko at gunpoint, and two officers cuffed him.

Tears of gratitude poured from Viktoria. She tried to speak but could only gasp and cough.

"We're here, baby," Aedan said, and he and Mackenzie wrestled with the straps around her wrists and ankles.

The moment Viktoria was free, Aedan scooped her into his arms, rocking her and stroking her hair. "Viki, are you okay? Tell me you're okay."

She nodded but still couldn't speak. Gripping his arms, she angled her face so she could meet his eyes. Finally, she was able to gasp out some words. "I'm me. I'm here."

"I see you," he replied and kissed her forehead, cheeks, and mouth. "I was afraid we were too late."

Tags rattled and Viktoria looked down. Puddles gazed up at her.

"Good boy. You found me, didn't you?" Her breathing had returned to normal, and, while her throat felt like she'd swallowed razor blades, she could speak without coughing. "Rowan helped me." She choked on a sob. "I made it back because Rowan pushed Talitha out of the way."

"I'll need to interview you, Miss Kovacs," Detective Baker said. "I've called paramedics to come and check you out, but then we need to talk."

"She's not up to it." Aedan's arms around Viktoria tightened.

"He needs me to tell him what happened, Aedan. I'll be okay."

He kissed the top of her head. "I'll stay with you."

"Me too," Mackenzie said.

Baker turned to Mackenzie. "I'll want to speak to you as well. You need to explain how you knew to send me here."

Mackenzie nodded. "No problem." She glanced reassuringly at Viktoria and turned back to Baker. "Whatever you need, Detective. Thank you for saving my friend."

Baker waved to the two officers, and they escorted Niko up the stairs. As he walked past Viktoria, his gaze locked onto hers.

"We'll be together eventually, darling."

Aedan went rigid and hissed out a breath.

"Ignore him," Viktoria said. "You're done, Niko. Talitha's gone. You'll never get her back." Impressions popped into her head. The source was Rowan, and the images verified Talitha had been removed to the spirit plane to face the consequences of her actions.

Niko simply smiled and let the police officers lead him away.

CHAPTER 33

Aedan's arm around her waist reassured Viktoria. The two made their way along the path to the front door of Aedan's house, Puddles romping along beside them.

"Thank the Goddess, it's over," Viktoria said. "Thank you for helping me."

"You're welcome." Aedan unlocked the door and ushered her inside. He guided her to the kitchen and didn't release her until she was settled on one of the bar stools by the island. Silently, he filled the kettle with water and plugged it in.

His expression was grim as he went through the motions of making tea.

Viktoria waited for him to speak, but when he placed a mug of tea in front of her, still without a word, she said, "What's wrong?"

"We need to talk."

Her pulse raced. "About what?"

He approached her and took her hands in his. "About what happened."

"Aedan, I just spent two hours reviewing it with Detective Baker. You were right there."

"I know," he said. "Bear with me."

Puddles nudged Aedan's leg, and he glanced down. A puzzled expression crossed Aedan's face. "Are you talking to him right now?"

Viktoria smiled. "No. But he wants you to tell him what a good job he did. You should reward him. He saved my life."

"You're right." Aedan released her hands and went to get the dog a biscuit. "Good job, Pud. You saved the day. Sit."

The dog sat, and after a moment, Aedan let him have the cookie. "All right, boy. Good dog." He patted Puddles on the head.

Distraction over, Aedan returned to Viktoria and took her hands again. "You almost died."

"Yes." Where was he going with this?

"I can't stand how close I came to losing you."

"It's okay. Niko's locked up. He won't be able to hurt anyone now."

"No, but the whole thing reminded me how life can change in a moment. I've avoided long-term relationships, Viki. My focus was my career and travel. The excitement made me feel alive. But since I've met you, I've realized I want more balance. I want a serious relationship, but I don't want just anyone. I want you." He lifted her from the chair and wrapped his arms around her.

Viktoria nuzzled her head against his shoulder, encircling him with her arms. "Me too, Aedan. Work was my life. Helping people, using my abilities, gave me fulfillment, but I've never had a serious relationship. I never wanted one." Over the years, her life had been full and exciting. And yet, she hadn't known it could be so much more. "When we're not together, I understand what loneliness is."

"Move in here, Viki. You and Walter." He put a finger under her chin and angled her face up.

She stared up at him, the wind knocked out of her.

"Say yes." He captured her lips, released them.

"Say yes." Again he kissed her, pulled up.

She smiled before he could go another round and said, "What if I say no?"

"I'll stalk you."

She laughed. "What if I get a restraining order and sic Detective Baker on you?"

Now he chuckled. "I'll pine away and die of a broken heart."

"Then I guess I'd better say yes."

His expression turned serious. "I love you, Viktoria."

She rose up on her toes to reach his lips. "I love you, Aedan."

A nudge between their legs made them each take a step back. Puddles gazed up at them, a question in his dark, intelligent eyes.

Together, Aedan and Viktoria said, "I love you, too, Puddles."

***

Niko awoke in the prison's infirmary and forced away the grin that had spread automatically on his face before the doctor noticed. He'd tricked his way in here with a mild heart attack.

The doctor was young—a suitable donor—but even if he hadn't been, Niko wouldn't have cared. What was that expression about beggars not being choosers? It would be difficult without Talitha to help him, but it wouldn't be impossible.

He closed his eyes. This would drain all his power, and he'd be weak

141

afterward.

The doctor moved to examine the patient's chart but felt a twinge in his chest. Pain radiated down his left arm, and he broke out in a sweat. Dizzy, he dropped the chart and gripped the bedrail. He tried to cry out, actually believed he had, though no sound had come from his gaping mouth.

He slid to the floor, dead.

In the bed, Niko visualized his own heart stopping. He mentally squeezed on it until it burst and his body went lax, the eyes staring into nothing.

A guard found the young doctor passed out on the floor and summoned help. They made sure the doctor was stabilized before they turned their attention to the man on the bed. It was obvious the patient was gone.

The young doctor, when he regained consciousness, couldn't explain what had happened. He had no recollection of finding the patient dead in bed or of having a heart attack. As a precaution, the room was quarantined and examined for toxic fumes, the patient's body and the doctor both tested for poison. After all, it was a pretty steep coincidence for two men to experience a heart attack simultaneously.

When the examinations were done, the young doctor picked up the chart and checked the name at the top—his name. He was Dr. Bernard Sanford. Perfect. A doctor would have respect, wouldn't be questioned leaving the country.

He would go to the doctor's residence, pack, and disappear to the Farkas home in Romania. It would be good to see his family again. Ah, poor Talitha. She was gone forever now. He couldn't bring her back from so far on the other side. It was a shame to lose her after so many centuries, but no sense in wasting time on what couldn't be changed.

Niko stepped from the hospital room. Time to begin his new life.

###

SAMPLE CHAPTER: *GILLIAN'S ISLAND*

Today, my life changes forever.

Gillian Foster unclipped the last clothes peg and hauled the crisp, white sheet from the line. It went into the laundry basket beside her with the rest of the bedding, all of it done for a man she'd never met.

As resort owner, she'd often done laundry for strangers when an extra pair of hands was needed, but this time, it was different. This time, it was for Daylin Quinn, the resort's new owner, and that made her every motion heavy and reluctant.

The heat didn't help put a spring in her step. The day was uncharacteristically hot, the air oppressive. It was the first of May and felt like the end of June.

Gillian sighed and ran her fingers through her hair, which always frizzed up in humidity. She bunched it into her fist to let a passing breeze cool her neck.

The wind that had dried her sheets so quickly would also blow in a cold front. The puffy, white clouds overhead now showed hints of grey. Sooner or later, a storm would blow in. Hopefully, it wouldn't be until after Daylin had arrived safely on the island—unless it rolled in fast.

Then she could use it to her advantage and delay the visit until tomorrow. Sure, it put off the inevitable, but a storm was a legitimate reason to procrastinate.

Gillian hefted the basket onto her hip and walked from the garden through the sunroom to the large living room. She set the basket on the floor and arched backward, rubbing her lower back.

A stereo system in the corner next to the fieldstone fireplace had a radio, and she switched it on. Eventually, there'd be a weather report.

Damn it, if she was forced to sell her home, why did it have to be to an arrogant developer like Daylin Quinn?

When he'd made the offer through his real estate agent, Gillian had researched him on the Internet. That had been both enlightening and infuriating.

He had a history of buying up properties, demolishing the buildings, and redeveloping the lots. It had made him a wealthy man, but the prospect of her beautiful century home being torn down nauseated her.

She envisioned a cheesy souvenir shop and tacky cabins; the porch swing gone, a snack machine in its place; the quaint restaurant preparing home-cooked meals replaced by greasy fast food. Her blood boiled as she imagined what he might do, and Gillian wished this city boy had stayed there despite how close to her asking price he'd come.

Most of the photos she'd found of him showed a stunningly handsome man with a variety of gorgeous women on his arm—sometimes one on each arm. No mention of a wife or steady girlfriend. Not that it was any of her business, but it was a reflection of his character.

Worse still, he was an American. A New Yorker.

The locals weren't pleased when the news that the Fosters had sold the island to a foreigner had spread. Most of them admitted no one living in the area had the millions required to buy the resort. Still, they considered it a betrayal that the purchaser not only wasn't from Ontario but wasn't even a Canadian.

No matter that Daylin's had been the only offer in the two years it had been on the market. Nor did anyone care that Gillian's ex-husband had forced her to sell so he could get his half of the money. Folks simply expressed their resentment at what she had done without regard to the extenuating circumstances.

Now Daylin was coming to claim what was legally his.

Gillian carried the laundry basket into the master bedroom to make the queen bed, one of the many pieces of furniture she was leaving here.

She'd already moved most of the possessions she was keeping into a storage unit on the mainland in the town of Fiddlehead. The meagre wardrobe and personal items she'd need for her month here had been transferred into a room in the staff quarters.

Daylin had contracted Gillian to stay on for two months to show him how the resort operated. She planned to live on the island for the first month and then move to the mainland and commute to work for the second month. This would help her transition to life without her island.

The scent of the outdoors wafted from the freshly laundered sheets as she worked. The cozy comforter she spread out on the bed would provide warmth for the remaining chilly nights ahead. She arranged the decorative pillows and stepped back to survey her handiwork.

All was ready.

Daylin would probably claim this room for his own until he destroyed the place.

Stop it. You don't know that's what he wants to do. She shook her head. It wasn't being cynical if history showed that's what he'd always done.

The weather report caught her attention. She cheered and did a skip-dance when the announcer upgraded the storm watch to a warning.

Gillian rushed to the kitchen where she'd left her cell phone and called Daylin's office.

His assistant answered and took the message. She assured Gillian she'd notify Mr. Quinn to stay in his hotel tonight and head out to the island the next morning.

Relief flooded through Gillian as she disconnected the call, and she sent a quick thank you to whatever weather god might be responsible for this turn. Admittedly, it was silly to get so excited over a one-night reprieve. Nevertheless, the rescheduling made her heart soar.

When Daylin stepped foot on shore, the place would be his. Until then, she'd spend tonight blessedly alone, curled up in front of the fireplace with a book and a glass of wine.

First, she'd better batten down the hatches before the storm hit.

***

Daylin Quinn ended his call and started his Mercedes-Benz E-Class sedan, which sat in the hotel parking lot. He gazed up at the sky.

The sun speared through grey-tinged clouds devoid of menace. His assistant had caught him in time to abort the trip to the island, but Daylin wouldn't let a little rain spoil his plans.

Rain seemed a remote possibility anyway, judging by the sky. If he was wrong, it might hit while he was crossing the channel between mainland and island, but so what? His boat was sturdy and would get him across.

He'd waited long enough to visit his new place again. The quick walk-through before he'd bought the island was a faint memory. He had big plans to implement, and the desire to get started was an itch he had to scratch right now.

To hell with rain. Most forecasts were wrong anyway.

Light traffic on the highway ensured he'd quickly get to the marina where he'd leave his car and pick up his boat. From there, it was ten minutes to the island.

Daylin looked forward to meeting Gillian Foster. He'd investigated the former owner of Loon Island Resort and liked what he'd seen.

She'd lovingly cared for the place even after her marriage had broken down and she'd been left to run it alone. Her insistence on putting into the sales contract a clause to honour the reservations she'd taken before the sale had impressed him. He'd agreed to it readily.

If he ran the resort this season, he'd get a feel for the land before he made any changes. The bonus was that her pictures showed a fit, sexy body despite her hiding it under sweatshirts and baggy pants.

As he sped toward the turnoff to Loon Island Marina Road, Daylin cranked the radio and burst into song. Anticipation and joy surged through him, and it was all he could do not to bounce on the seat like a kid on Santa's knee. The start of an important new project always gave him a thrill, and he was on his way to meet with an intriguing new woman.

Could it get any better than this?

###

ABOUT THE AUTHOR

Val Tobin lives in Newmarket, Ontario, with her husband, Bob, and Scully, their cat. After ten years in the computer industry programming web and software apps, she now spends her days writing, reading, and searching for the perfect butter tart. Her educational background includes a diploma in Computer Information Systems from DeVry Toronto, a B.Sc. in Parapsychic Science from the American Institute of Holistic Theology, a M.Sc. in Parapsychology from AIHT, Reiki Master/Teacher certifications, and Angel Therapy Practitioner® certifications.

Val's website: http://www.serenitynowgifts.com/

Other Books by Val Tobin

Fiction

SF Thrillers

The Valiant Chronicles Series

Earthbound (prequel): A spirit becomes earthbound after refusing to cross over in order to solve her murder and prevent more deaths, some of which might be predestined. Get *Earthbound* and learn what came before.

The Experiencers (book one): A black-ops assassin atones for his brutal past by helping an alien abductee escape capture. Get *The Experiencers* to start your experience.

A Ring of Truth (Book Two): A rogue assassin attempts to rescue a group of alien abductees and triggers Armageddon.

The Valiant Chronicles books are also available as a box set in e-book and paperback.

Romantic Suspense

Injury: A young actress at the height of her career has her personal life turned upside down when a horrifying family secret makes front-page news.

Gillian's Island: A socially anxious divorcée confronts her greatest fears when she's forced to sell her island home and falls for the dashing new owner. Visit *Gillian's Island* now.

About Three Authors: Poison Pen: Three wannabe authors suffering from various mental disorders find love in unexpected places when they interfere in the investigation of a colleague's murder. For a generous helping of romance and murder, get *Poison Pen.*

Forever Young: You Again: Complications arise when an accounting tech is assigned her former lover as a client and his company's previous financial controller is found dead. Love, loss, and second chances. Get *You Again* now.

Paranormal Romance

Walk-In: A young psychic woman fights an attraction to a handsome but sceptical novelist while she battles a power-hungry sorcerer determined to make her his next conquest. Get *Walk-In* now to start the magick and madness.

Horror Suspense

The Hunted: A Storm Lake Story: A monster hunter revisits her terrifying past while helping a reporter uncover the origins of Storm Lake's creatures. A stand-alone sequel to the short story "Storm Lake," *The Hunted* takes place twelve years later. Get *The Hunted* now to confront Storm Lake's monsters.

Urban Fantasy

Tales from the Unmasqued World Series

The Fool: New Beginnings (Book One): A newly divorced woman suffering a midlife crisis gets involved in the search for a missing half-vampire teen. Get *The Fool* now and step into the unmasqued world.

The Magician: Infinity's End (Book Two): After getting expelled for setting a demon loose on campus, a student mage searches for the real culprit and finds his troubles have only just begun.

The High Priestess: Persephone's Return: Stuck in the spirit world, Jaycie struggles to find a way out before it's too late. But others want to keep her there forever. Will she make it out of Hades alive?